Praise for *Kelvin McClo*

"*Kelvin McCloud and the Seaside Storm* enables its readers to learn about the workings of our atmosphere through an engaging and entertaining story. Michael Erb has used his knowledge of meteorology to craft a "whodunit" that will motivate the reader to think more deeply about what happens in the sky above us."

- Dr. Tony Broccoli, Professor, Rutgers University

"This book is an entertaining whodunit tale. The reader will be captivated by the adventures of young Henry, his friend Rachel and his uncle as they piece together a murderous meteorological puzzle. Weather events play a prominent role in the story and author Erb weaves many an educational lesson into the narrative, making it fun for a young reader to become more weatherwise."

- Dr. David Robinson, Professor & New Jersey State Climatologist, Rutgers University

KELVIN MCCLOUD
AND THE SEASIDE STORM

For information, write to: Tumblehome Learning, 201 Newton Street Weston, MA USA 02493, www.tumblehomelearning.com

Library of Congress Control Number: 2012935950

Erb, Michael.
Kelvin McCloud and the Seaside Storm / Michael Erb.
ISBN 978-0-9850008-3-7

1. Children - Fiction 2. Mystery 3. Science 4. Weather 5. Meteorology

Cover Art: Evelyn Schwartzhauer
Cover Design: Carrie Rogers
Illustrations: Susan Paquette

Printed in the USA by Corporate Graphics, North Mankato, MN.

10 9 8 7 6 5 4 3 2 1

KELVIN MCCLOUD
AND THE SEASIDE STORM

Michael Erb

TUMBLEHOME learning

For Mom, Dad, and Julie

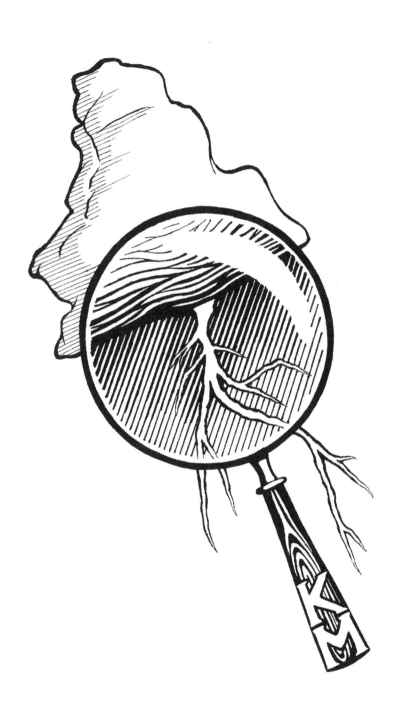

Table of Contents

Chapter One

The Weather Detective

The hairs on Henry Alabaster's arms bristled when he heard the sound outside his bedroom door that night. It was one long, quiet creak, like an old stair complaining under too much weight.

Henry looked up from the photo in his hands. The small lamp on his desk didn't illuminate much more than him and the crumpled white sheets over his raised knees, leaving the door on the near wall in partial darkness. Somewhere outside, the long creak petered out. Was it his uncle? No, the occasional purr of snoring continued down the hall.

Henry set the picture frame back on his desk, returning his missing parents to their usual spot. Beside their two smiling faces, the dim numbers of Henry's spaceship alarm clock radiated the time: two fourteen a.m.

Henry clicked off the lamp and slid his legs out of bed, touching down gingerly on his toes.

His foot brushed a stack of comics, toppling them over. Another sound came from the next room: a soft, quick scrape. Henry paused. Then, easing his bedroom door open an inch, he put his eye to the gap.

City lights shimmered on the living room ceiling. A broken ribbon of light shone at the base of the apartment's front door, outlining the shapes of furniture and old bookshelves.

Henry blinked. Nobody was in the living room. Not a cat burglar or a spy or even one of those lanky gray aliens they sometimes showed on the sci-fi channel. He opened his door wider. One of those alien shows was on TV last night, he remembered. *Aliens Throughout History*, it was called, and it featured grainy footage of a long-limbed figure standing with President Truman way back at the end of World War II. The show's eerie music had made everything in the apartment seem sinister, and the scariness remained there now in the quiet room. Even his uncle's snores and the muffled city sounds coming in at the window didn't help. This late at night, everything seemed sinister.

Henry scanned the room again. His night vision had started to kick in, and this time he did spot something. A small, thick envelope lay on the floor, half illuminated by the yellow light sneaking under the door. Its stark white surface contrasted sharply with the dark floorboards. Who'd put that there?

No deliveryman came at this time of night. Well, maybe a ninja deliveryman, but not a regular one. Henry took two steps into the living room. The long, slow, shuddering creak came again from just outside the front door. Henry froze. Two shadows cut the light at the bottom of the door.

Henry heard himself breathing. For once this creaky old place had been useful. That spot in the hallway always creaked when someone stepped on it the wrong way. The shadows darted to the right and vanished.

Henry ran for the door. The envelope still lay on the floor, with a bit of elegant, looping cursive scrawled on the front, but Henry had no time for that now. Flinging himself into the suddenly bright hallway, he glimpsed something yellow at the end of the corridor. No, not just yellow, but a woman— a tall woman with long blond hair and a yellow summer dress—vanishing into the stairwell.

Who was that? No alien Henry ever saw. He sprinted after her, pushed into the stairwell at the end of the hall, and stared downward through all of the dizzying, circling sections of concrete steps. He couldn't see the woman, but her faint, quick footsteps echoed back to him from somewhere far below. He circled downward after her. The footsteps didn't get closer. Somewhere ahead, a door shut.

Several floors lower, Henry pushed through a heavy steel door and felt a wave of muggy summer air on his face. In front of him, dark streets tinted with yellow light stretched between the buildings of Midtown West, Manhattan. Or Hell's Kitchen, as it was normally called. Henry stopped, his feet aching. Trying to catch his breath, he looked around.

No luck. The woman was gone. Henry glanced at the sky, imagining a UFO zipping away above the rooftops.

He shook his head. "Grow up," he said to nobody in particular.

Henry closed his eyes, picturing that long yellow hair again, vanishing into the stairwell. It stirred something in him. It felt as if a serpent had just woken up in his gut and now slithered and coiled inside him. Who was that woman? Something about that hair...

A group of teens wearing baggy T-shirts walked by, hands deep in their pockets. Henry turned back inside. The grimy stairwell seemed cool compared to the muggy summer night, and Henry started the long walk up the stairs in silence.

Ninth floor. In the hallway ahead, a polished mahogany plaque hung next to his uncle's apartment door. Henry had helped his uncle hang it there last winter, and it was the only thing that looked new in this dirty old place. Silver letters stood out from the dark surface. It read:

Kelvin McCloud
Weather Detective

Engraved above the words, the plaque bore a small image of a thunderstorm covered by a magnifying lens.

Next to this, framed in the open doorway, stood Henry's uncle—a tall, thin man wearing a deep blue bathrobe over his cloud-patterned pajamas. He held the small white envelope from the floor, torn open, in one hand. His other hand contained a newspaper clipping.

Kelvin's sharp gray eyes gleamed.

"What is it?" Henry asked.

Kelvin raised his long eyebrows, and the corners of his mouth curled upward into a smile.

"It's just what we've been waiting for," he said. He tapped the newspaper clipping a few times with his finger. "A mystery."

Henry's skin tingled. The word was electric. Mystery. Ever since opening this weather detective business six months ago, they'd been waiting for something like this. Not the howling windows and leaking roofs of fussy neighbors, but an honest-to-goodness mystery.

Turning, Kelvin crossed their dark living room in four long strides and disappeared into his study. Closing the apartment door, Henry followed. There was quickness in his uncle's step, the clear sign that some scientific curiosity tingled on his brain. Kelvin was a reserved man about most things, and he could seem terse and confrontational about subjects that didn't interest him, but he had a clear love of solving problems.

Kelvin flipped on the study's lamp, which cast a soft cone of light across a desk cluttered with books, papers, and metal and glass contraptions. Henry and Kelvin's shadows fell across tall shelves of science books. The books bore titles like *Paleoclimatology* and *Physical Oceanography* and lent the small room a musty smell of leather and old paper. A small cot with rumpled sheets occupied one half of the room.

Kelvin cast off his slippers and pushed the books and papers on his desk aside, careful not to break any of the thermometers, barometers, or cup anemometers sitting there. A grin spread beneath his bent, hawkish nose. In the open space on his desk, he placed the small white envelope. The envelope, Henry now saw, still had something in it.

"Now just you look at that," Kelvin said, giving the envelope a rapid tap with his finger. Leaning in, Henry read the looping cursive on the front.

To Kelvin McCloud:
Something you should look into. –S.

Henry nodded. A good start. He lifted the torn

edge of the envelope to see inside, and then drew back with a sharp breath.

"Holy crap! What's that?"

Kelvin smiled. "Hundred dollar bills. Ten of them."

"Yeah, but what for?"

"Advance payment for the case, I would think."

Kelvin set the newspaper clipping on the desk and Henry peered around his uncle's shoulder. A grainy black and white portrait sat beside a column of blocky text. The portrait showed an older gentleman with a sagging neck but sharp, intelligent eyes.

Above the picture, the headline ran, *Local Banker Killed by Sleetstone.* Despite the oppressive heat of the dark study, a chill ran through Henry.

"Did you get a good look at the woman, Henry?"

"Uh, not really. She was—" Henry stopped, thunderstruck. "Wait. You were snoring. How'd you..."

"How'd I know it was a woman?" Kelvin looked at him with a knowing smile, and Henry immediately realized how foolish his question was.

"Well, for one, the handwriting." Kelvin pressed down a long finger on the envelope. "See? Men rarely write with such flourish. Now, this could have been dropped off by a man, but considering the writer's apparent desire for secrecy, I deemed the possibility unlikely. And two—" He pressed down a second finger and here gave a small, embarrassed shrug of his shoulders. "A few strands of long blond hair lay on the hallway floor. She must have lingered outside our door for a moment, pulling on her hair, probably debating her decision to come here. So did you see her?"

"Just a little. Like you said, she had blond hair. Yellow dress. She was about your age: mid-forties. That's all I could see." Henry pointed to the ornate S on the front of the envelope. "An initial, you think?"

Kelvin held the envelope up to the desk lamp, leaning forward to inspect it at close range. It cast a huge rectangular shadow over much of the small room. "Very likely. Look out for people with S names, I suppose?"

Henry's attention returned to the newspaper clipping. That's what he really wanted to see. Man, a thousand bucks, for what? Dead of night, nearly two-forty now, and his mind buzzed with the possibilities of what might be in that article. "So, what's it say?"

Kelvin followed Henry's gaze. He smiled. Adjusting the lamp, he slid the article closer. "Well, why don't you tell me?"

Henry took the article and, hands trembling, began to read.

Chapter Two

The Sleetstone Case

Local Banker Killed by Sleetstone
Sandy Run, N.J. – The body of local banker
Edward J. Wrightly was discovered lying face down
in the grass in front of his house on Browning Lane
this morning, following a violent storm that swept
through Sandy Run during the night.
Wrightly was spotted by a neighbor at 6:15 a.m.,
surrounded by the remains of white, nickel-sized
sleetstones from last night's storm. Eyewitnesses
report that severe bruising covered much of his
body, and a medical team pronounced him dead at
the scene. According to police speculation, Wrightly
may have attempted to reach his front door when
he arrived home in the storm, whereupon he was
fatally struck in the back of the head by the falling
ice. No foul play is suspected.
Edward Wrightly, 63, worked for 40 years at
Oceanside Banking and Loan, where he rose to

the position of executive vice president. He quickly became one of the town's most wealthy residents, and the seaside manor where he lived is one of the largest residences in the town.

"Ed was pretty well liked around here," said neighbor Josephina Rosenbloom. "We didn't see him too often, but he was quick with a smile. He was bright, too. It's such a shame for this to happen."

Wrightly's seaside estate and fortune are to be divided according to his will, the particulars of which are unknown. He is survived by no children.

Henry lowered the paper. Was that all? He turned to the back, only to see part of an unrelated story about watermelons. The top of the page displayed the name of the newspaper, The Daily Conch, dated yesterday.

Kelvin sat on the edge of his desk, peering at Henry. "So?"

The word hung in the stillness of the tiny room. Henry didn't know what to say. "It's too bad, I guess."

"Too bad?"

"Yeah, the guy sounds all right. Too bad he died."

Kelvin, brushing the comment away with a wave, said, "Yes, yes, undoubtedly. But what do you think of the circumstances? The 'sleetstones'?"

Something seemed off to Henry about the sleetstones. Kelvin had explained all about sleet

Henry reading

last January. Henry checked the article again: nickel-sized sleetstones.

The answer clicked into place. "That can't be right."

Kelvin prodded. "How so?"

"Well, sleet just can't get that big. Sleet is frozen rain, so it has to be raindrop size. That's way smaller than a nickel. Plus, sleet doesn't usually happen in the summer. The article must be talking about hail."

Kelvin smiled. "Precisely. That's the first thing I noticed too, but it may be a simple mix-up by the writer. If you're not familiar with these things, it's easy to get hail and sleet confused. However, there are other things that don't make sense."

Henry eyed the article again, but he couldn't see anything unusual.

Standing up, Kelvin turned to his bookshelf. He passed his fingers over the thick volumes. "Take, for instance, the death itself. The article suggests he was killed by hail, but how large does it say the hail was?"

"Nickel-sized."

Kelvin picked a nickel off the bookshelf and tossed it to Henry. It didn't look big enough to kill a man.

"Ah, and here!" Kelvin dislodged a well-worn volume. He paged through it, stopping somewhere near the back. "Deaths by hail," he read aloud. "In the United States, only a handful of hail-related deaths have occurred since 1900. One is the tragic case of... Let's skip forward a little. Here we are. In most deaths involving hail, the hailstones reached the size of baseballs or larger. The largest hailstone ever found in the U.S. measured eight inches across."

Kelvin snapped the book shut. Henry eyed the nickel in his hand. It looked miniscule. And eight inches across! That sounded more like a cantaloupe.

"What about the broken windows?" Henry asked. "The dented house? Enough hailstones could kill somebody. It didn't have to be a single blow."

Kelvin fixed him with a stare. "Henry, I'm not saying hail isn't dangerous. It is. Don't ever let yourself be caught out in a hailstorm. But the article doesn't say he was killed by a lot of little bruises. What does it say?"

"Struck in the back of the head... and killed."

Kelvin nodded. "Not many blows, but one. Doesn't sound much like an accident, does it?"

Henry's response died before it reached his lips. His uncle was right. Suddenly, it didn't sound much like an accident at all. As Henry stood in the study with his uncle, a suffocating feeling rose from the recesses of his stomach.

For a moment, Henry didn't think about the case, but about the past: before he and his uncle started this weather detective business, before he moved to New York City, back to when he lived in Pennsylvania with his parents. The images from that wretched day still cut into him. They seemed bright and unreal, like a movie played on lousy projection. He recalled the school bus receding down the green lane by his house. He remembered those noisy squirrels leaping from branch to branch in the great maple trees out front, knocking down leaves. Then that man and woman in their stuffy gray suits came to the door. They used no pleasantries, but simply explained to Henry that Susan and Arthur, his parents, were missing.

Not dead, they said—at least not for sure—but missing.

Missing after their plane disappeared over the Atlantic. What did that even mean?

Henry blinked. He found Kelvin staring at him. Concern creased his uncle's face. "What's wrong, Henry?"

Henry's stomach churned, twisting around itself like a snake uncoiling.

"Look," Kelvin said, "about your parents. I know that—"

Henry didn't let him finish. "I know!" The words rung loudly in the small room. "I don't need to hear it. Let's just... could we not talk about that? I'm okay."

"You sure? Are you still having the night terrors?"

"Look, Kelvin, I'm okay."

Kelvin leaned against the bookshelf. He stayed silent for ten or fifteen seconds, pressing his lips together. "All right, Henry. Another time."

Henry discovered he was gripping the newspaper article with white knuckles. He placed it back on the desk. His stomach gradually unclenched.

"So what now? We go to Sandy Run?"

Kelvin corrected him. "I go to Sandy Run."

"But..."

"Remember, Henry, I'm the detective. You're," he added with a poke to the chest, "thirteen. If school was in session, you'd be studying algebra."

Henry clenched his fists. "And if you hadn't gotten fired, you'd still be at the university."

Kelvin cringed, but didn't respond; he said instead, "So what can I do with you? You could stay with your friend from baseball. Doug, was it?"

"He's visiting family."

"Really? Too bad. How about Mrs. Forrester? You remember her, right, from the Christmas party?"

Henry rolled his eyes. "She smells like cheese."

His uncle laughed, and then stifled it with a snort.

"Look," Henry said, "there's no way I'm staying here. I helped all the times you wanted to put up signs and pass out fliers. We're in this together."

Kelvin met his nephew's gaze. "Of course you're right. We're in this together. But if things get dangerous, you're staying at the hotel."

Being stuck at a hotel didn't sound like much fun, but now wasn't the time to haggle. "Fine. So what about the woman? What do we do about her?"

Kelvin slipped the envelope and article into his bathrobe pocket and stretched his arms. "Our client? Nothing. She gave us a case. She paid. Now we look into Wrightly's death. But keep in mind, Henry— and this is important—that we're not sure he was murdered. That's not how an investigation works. It's just a hypothesis for now. The hypothesis comes first, then the evidence. Evidence is paramount. We'll figure out what really happened once we get down there."

Kelvin clicked off the light. As Henry left the room, excitement pounded in his chest. Finally, a mystery. The first real case for him and his uncle, the weather detective.

Henry paused at his bedroom door. "So when do we leave?"

The answer came out of the darkness. "Tomorrow, as soon as we're awake. After all, for a summertime mystery, the last thing you want is for the case to go cold."

Chapter Three

The Silver Barometer

Henry leaned back and kicked his feet up on the dashboard, fanning himself with a pamphlet he found in the glove box. All week had been like this: swelteringly hot no matter where you were, and the shade from the towering office buildings filing past outside did little to help. The car gurgled and bumped as Kelvin drove, and Henry tapped his toe in time with the sounds.

They had meant to be out of the city by nine that morning. Now a distant church bell rang out five o'clock, and they had just gotten on their way.

They'd had car trouble. Not the usual getting-a-flat-tire kind, but the jolting, grinding, I-think-something-just-fell-off kind. A mechanic got the old beater back up and running, though, and finally they were on the road. As soon as more money from these cases started coming in, Kelvin promised, they'd get a new car, but for now this would have to do.

That would be the day, Henry thought. Maybe a sleek red sports car. And a bit of AC would do wonders. Funny, Henry thought: Kelvin McCloud, weather detective, didn't even have climate control.

Still, there was no point in blaming Kelvin for something like that. Supporting an extra person in New York City wasn't an easy task for anyone, Henry knew, and certainly not for an ex-professor with dwindling savings. Henry remained grateful he had a bed to sleep in at all. After all, for the past eight months, Kelvin had slept on a cot in the study.

Henry's thoughts lingered on his uncle's study. Everything that had happened last night—the mysterious woman, the money, the obituary—still made his arms tingle and his mind race, and he wondered how all of the pieces of this mystery would fit together. It was like a puzzle, which was good, because Henry loved puzzles. It was a passion he'd shared with his parents, back in Pennsylvania. Thursdays had been puzzle night, where he and his parents would take puzzles, brain-teasers, and games of all sorts from the cabinets and sit on the soft carpet to work through them together.

Henry remembered, vividly, the clap on the back from Dad and the bright, joyous laugh from Mom whenever he solved a particularly hard riddle or won a whodunit board game.

Henry shook that thought out of his head. A thin silver chain hung from the corner of Kelvin's pants pocket, attached to a belt loop. Henry had seen it before. On the other end, he knew, hidden in Kelvin's pocket, hung an odd silver and glass device.

"Brought your barometer, huh?"

Kelvin patted the pocket. "Wouldn't leave home without it."

Henry remembered seeing the barometer sitting on Kelvin's desk on the day he moved in, eight months ago. It looked a bit like an old pocket watch, but it didn't tell the time. It wasn't until months later that Kelvin explained how it helped predict the weather.

Would it be useful in Sandy Run? Henry couldn't say, but why go to a weather detective unless you have a weather mystery? Staring out the window, Henry pictured the evening Kelvin told him about the barometer.

"You wouldn't know it," Kelvin said, "but the sky is heavy."

The comment surprised Henry. Not only because it was an unusual thing to say, but because they hadn't been talking about the sky at all. They were just walking down West 42nd Street after some cheery musical at the Westside Theater when Kelvin stopped and pulled the device out of a breast pocket.

"Look at this, Henry," he said, kneeling down. Lights from nearby stores provided the instrument with a steady silver shine despite the coming nightfall. As if the device was a clock, a thin metal hand lay beneath well-worn glass, circled by sets of numbers. "Mind if I tell you about something?"

Henry shook his head.

"Good. It's about the atmosphere, something that fascinated me when I was a kid. Still does, really. Atmosphere means, quite literally, 'vapor sphere.' It protects us from harmful space radiation and gives us air to breathe, and it pushes in on us all of the time. We're just so used to it we don't even notice. This device, this barometer, is like a scale. It measures how much air is above us."

Henry remembered being intrigued by this. He had never known his uncle very well, Kelvin being one of those relatives you only see once every other year. Henry leaned forward, listening intently.

"The trick," Kelvin said with a grin, "is in watching how the pressure of the air—that's a measure of how much air is above us—changes. All over the world, air moves around. For us in the United States, warm air comes from the south and cold air comes from the north. These bodies of air mix and push each other all the time, like water mixing in the ocean. This results in changes in the wind and also leads to slightly more air being over some places and less over others. These pressure changes are important, and when the pressure somewhere is high or low, we call that a high or a low. You've probably heard about those on TV."

Henry nodded. The weather people on TV did sometimes mention highs and lows, but Henry never knew exactly why he should care.

"Well," Kelvin went on, "highs and lows form and dissipate slowly, and they move across the world. They move from the Pacific Ocean to the Atlantic, from Hong Kong to Hawaii. The highs can be important, but lows are more exciting. Lows can bring all sorts of interesting weather with them. Rain, strong wind, sometimes thunder and lightning, maybe some hail, that sort of thing. Since this device tells you about the air pressure, all you have to do is check where that little needle points. It's not perfect, but it gives you some idea of what's coming. Fair weather or foul."

Henry stared with wide eyes. "Could I see it?"

Kelvin slipped the fancy silver one back into his pocket, but handed Henry a simpler one to keep.

That was six months ago. Sitting in the sweltering car, Henry reached into his backpack and pulled out his simple barometer. The back was plain and didn't have an inscription like Kelvin's, but he liked it. He liked seeing a hint of what the future might hold. Under the glass, the needle pointed far to the right. High pressure.

"No storms today."

"No," his uncle agreed. "Just heat."

As they plunged into the fluorescent lights of the Lincoln Tunnel, Henry hefted the barometer in his hand. It had a bit of weight to it, and he imagined he was holding a big, wet, cold hailstone. Could something like that have killed a man? Henry pictured that terrible, howling storm. It came with a huge low, no doubt. If Mr. Wrightly had owned a barometer, or listened to the weather at all, maybe he'd still be alive today.

A glare of sunlight distracted Henry from his dark, icy thoughts. Putting his feet down, he sat up. Out in front, the gray highway stretched into New Jersey, the Garden State.

Henry watched other cars zip by to their sides. "How long will it take to get there?"

Kelvin adjusted the mirror and shifted in his seat. "About an hour, I'd say. We'll be there before you know it."

Henry leaned back again and thought.

Sandy Run. What in the world would they find there?

Chapter Four

The Sandy Run Inn

At just past six o'clock Kelvin pulled the car to a stop. In front of them sat a building unlike any Henry had seen before. It was not a very tall building, nor very wide, but it seemed to be put together entirely with wrong angles and parts that didn't quite match. It looked as if a dozen different houses and shops had been nailed together, and this was the result.

At the front, above glass double doors, hung a sign: The Sandy Run Inn. Kelvin clicked off the ignition.

"Strange looking place," Henry said.

Kelvin nodded. "Only hotel with a vacancy."

Grabbing his backpack, Henry followed his uncle to the entrance, where a small brass bell atop the door chimed as they entered. A short, balding man sat behind a large reception desk.

"Good day," he said with a grimace. "How may

I help you?"

Kelvin set down his suitcase. They'd need a room for two, he said. Three nights, maybe longer. Would that be a problem?

The short man flipped a few pages in a book while rubbing his nose. His blue vest displayed a white nametag: Mr. Pen, proprietor. Without a word, he dropped from his stool and trudged into a back room.

Henry turned away. The lobby of the hotel, unlike the little man who ran it, provided a touch of grandeur. A large elevator stood beside a blue-carpeted stairwell. Large uncut tree-trunk crossbeams supported an elaborate chandelier. Floral wallpaper covered three of the walls, while the fourth was adorned with oil paintings in thick, garish frames.

Henry approached one of these paintings. It portrayed an old ship, sails strained with wind, charging headlong through a storm. White breakers crashed against the prow and dark clouds swirled overheard. Nearby, a dark waterspout threatened to bear down upon the crew, who worked busily to prepare for the worst.

Henry imagined himself on that beleaguered ship, feeling the wind and water whipping through the air. *Avast, secure that line*, he yelled. If they couldn't get the sails under control in time, this storm could be the death of them all. And to think,

just yesterday a favorable westerly gale had helped them round the Cape of Good Hope. Alas, such was the turbulent love affair between sailors, the sea, and the weather.

The innkeeper returned, and Henry let his seafaring fantasy slip away. "Sign here... and here..." Mr. Pen grumbled, "and then we'll just—"

The bell on the hotel door chimed. Three people entered the lobby, crossing toward the stairs. In front walked a tall, brightly dressed woman with dark ebony skin. She chatted with a tired-looking man, who waddled as he kept pace with her confident strides. Trailing them at some distance was a younger girl, her skin the shade of milk chocolate and her black hair done up in a ponytail with a light blue scrunchie. She looked about Henry's age. As the group passed, the girl glanced in Henry's direction.

Henry jumped. Should he be staring?

The girl pointed at the woman leading the way, made an exaggerated talking motion with her hand, and rolled her eyes.

"All right, we're all set."

Henry looked toward his uncle's voice. Kelvin strode toward the elevator, two keycards in hand.

"Let's check out our room. Third floor."

Henry turned back. The girl had disappeared. Disappointment nagged at him for a moment, but he joined his uncle at the elevator. The doors slid open to the sounds of smooth jazz.

"And no candles!" Mr. Pen shouted as they stepped inside the elevator. He leaned forward over his desk, glaring at them from across the room. "No fire at all. I hate fire. If you even think of—"

"Sure, sure," Kelvin said, jabbing the close-door button. The doors slid shut. "Insufferable man."

"So what's the plan?"

Kelvin tapped a foot against the ground. "Well, I wanted to visit the police station today, but it's too late for that. How about we take a jaunt to Wrightly's estate instead?"

Henry spun toward his uncle. "We can do that?"

"I don't see why not."

With a chime, the elevator door slid open to reveal a narrow, winding corridor. Hauling their luggage, Henry and Kelvin headed deeper into one of the many wings of the hotel. After a turn, the wallpaper changed from flowers to paisley and, somewhat alarmingly, the ceiling became half an inch lower.

They found room 327. The door stuck, but gave after Kelvin put his shoulder to it. TV. Two beds. Ugly plaid curtains. No surprises. Henry and Kelvin put down their things and left.

On their way back through the lobby, Kelvin strode past the front desk, then stopped and turned back. The hotel owner leafed through a magazine, clearly trying to ignore him.

"Ah, Mr. Pen," Kelvin said brightly, "we're going out for dinner."

Mr. Pen didn't look up. "That so?"

"Do you have any suggestions?"

"No."

Kelvin drummed his fingers on the desk. "I have a question, Mr. Pen. On the way down here I heard something on the radio. Well, uh, I forget the details, but did someone really die here in Sandy Run?"

Henry stared at his uncle. This wasn't normal. What was he up to? Across the desk, Mr. Pen's eyes lit up. "You mean old Ed Wrightly! Yes, you heard true. He got himself killed in a storm."

Of course, Henry thought. He hid a smile, realizing his uncle's ploy. Acting a bit like a fool could be a valuable strategy in an investigation. He joined Kelvin at the desk, playing along. "Wait, what happened?"

Kelvin turned to him, his long eyebrows raised above wide eyes. "Someone died, apparently."

Mr. Pen grinned, setting down his glossy magazine. "Happened in a thunderstorm just a few days ago, if you can believe it. Died not ten feet from his front door, the rich fool." The sound that came from Mr. Pen's mouth after he said these words sounded more like a snort than a laugh. "Lightning and hail got pretty heavy that evening. Ed got home and a hailstone caught him right in the back of the head. Crack." The short man slammed a palm down on the varnished desk. "Happened right around nine fifteen that night, when the storm was at its worst. Why he got home from work that late I can't say, and don't really care."

Henry nodded. "Didn't he have any protection? An umbrella, at least?"

"An umbrella? Yeah, I guess he did. They found it blown up against a neighbor's house, I think, torn to bits."

Kelvin shook his head, a solemn expression drooping over his face like a curtain. "Well it's a shame."

Mr. Pen blew a huff of air out of his nose. "A shame? Far from it. If he treated others like he treated me, I'd say he got what he deserved."

"What do you mean?" Henry asked.

Mr. Pen rolled his eyes. "Well, so, Ed was a banker, right? Some bigwig in charge of loans and stuff. And here I was, working myself to the bone last year to get this place into its current majestic state. And I may have missed a payment or two, and the collectors were banging on my door. Well okay, no big deal, I said, I'll just get another loan and pay it back once the business picks up. And do you know what? Our late friend Ed Wrightly turned me away. He told me this place violated some code or something. He said it wasn't fit to be a hotel and should be torn down!"

Mr. Pen's small chest heaved rapidly up and down, but he didn't stop for a moment.

"Can you believe it? This beauty of a place? It's been in the Pen family for years, and he wanted to tear it down! I lost my hair making sure that didn't happen, and I'll do whatever else it takes to keep this place running. That old man, or anyone else, isn't going to take it away from me."

Kelvin remained quiet for a few seconds. "Maybe you're right. Maybe he had it coming."

Mr. Pen sat on his tall swivel stool, eyeing them. "That's karma for you."

Henry wanted to shudder. His parents had always taught him to be a decent person. Didn't Mr. Pen ever have parents? Henry clenched his fists and asked another question. "The guy was rich, right? Anything get stolen that night?"

Mr. Pen rolled his eyes. "I don't think so, kid. Hail doesn't usually steal things."

Mr. Pen laughed, and Henry and Kelvin joined in. Then, bidding him goodbye, they left. The door chimed shut as they walked out into the warm late afternoon air.

Kelvin shook his head. "Didn't I tell you? Insufferable."

Chapter Five

The Dead Man's Estate

Outside Henry's open window, the shops and restaurants of Sandy Run slid by along a street lined with trees; he saw a convenience store, then a barbershop with a red and white spiral column, and then a burger joint with laughing kids out front, which made him hungry and eager for friends his own age.

Henry leaned back and let his arm hang out the window as he inhaled the saltwater and seaweed-scented air. Everything about this town was different from New York. It felt nice to escape the suffocating bustle and traffic of the city.

"Where now?" Kelvin asked.

Henry glanced at the directions. "Right on McKinley." Kelvin turned right. A park with slides and swings came into view. Farther on, Henry saw another park, this one for dogs. A tiny Maltese, yapping constantly, chased an Irish setter across the grass. Henry and Kelvin then passed into a residential area, heading for the ocean.

Henry pulled his arm inside the car. The air had been warm by the hotel, but the more they neared their destination, the cooler it got.

Kelvin glanced at him. "Got the shivers?"

Henry shook his head. Visiting a dead man's house wasn't exactly a vacation, but this feeling was more than just his nerves. The air had gotten cooler.

Hadn't Kelvin told him something about this once? Yes, it had to do with the ocean. Water takes longer to heat than land, so air above water doesn't get as warm.

And wasn't there something else? Now he remembered. Since warm air rises and cool air sinks, the warm air over the land goes up and the cooler air from the ocean blows in to replace it. Kelvin called this wind a sea breeze, because it came from the sea. It helped keep places near the coast cooler during the summer. Henry had never felt it back in Pennsylvania because they were too far from the ocean.

Henry thought about Pennsylvania. There, he and his parents were affected by the wind in a different way. On days when the wind blew more from the north, from up near Canada, it brought cooler air. When the wind blew more from the south, it brought warmer air. He figured that most places far from the ocean were like that.

Henry continued to stare out the window. "No, not shivers," he answered belatedly. "It's just the sea breeze."

Still, Henry couldn't shake the feeling that this cool air, coming in from the ocean, was the sign of something sinister. The cry of seagulls soon became audible over the wind rushing by the window.

"Beach is rougher on this side of town," Kelvin said. "Fewer houses, too."

Henry watched the houses speed by. A few sat off to the right—cheery, weather-worn residences in shades of pastel and brown—but on the other side stood nothing but tall grass and sand dunes. Just over those dunes lay the Atlantic Ocean. Henry couldn't see it yet, but he could hear it.

A grin grew on Kelvin's face. "Ah, there it is."

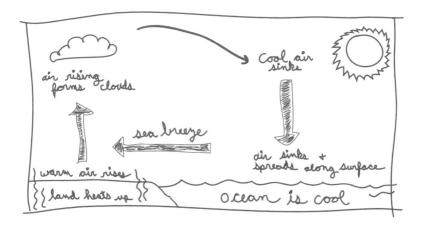

Ahead, another house came into view. But this house didn't look anything like the others. It looked more like a mansion. Even from a distance, Henry could see large bay windows, elegant gables, and high, dark-shingled spires sprouting from the top. The sand-colored, two-story manor stood alone on a slight rise by the beach, the pale afternoon sky outlining its striking design.

"Wow, what a place to live!" Henry said.

"Undoubtedly," Kelvin agreed, "but no place to die."

The car jostled past a white mailbox with **Wrightly** painted on the side. Kelvin turned into the long driveway. Ahead, the ocean spread out behind the expansive estate, a dark blue beneath the vast sky.

Next to the house, a black luxury sedan sat parked in an open-air car shelter.

"Hey, someone's already here," Henry said.

"No, I suspect that's Wrightly's car."

Yes, of course. The dead man's car. How comforting. Henry turned his eyes to the house again. Up close, it looked different. Cracked and broken windowpanes made some of the windows look like jagged-toothed mouths gaping open.

"Damaged in the hailstorm, no doubt," Kelvin said.

Kelvin pulled forward and turned off the engine. Just outside Henry's window, the black sedan stood like a dark tombstone. Ugly dents marred the roof and hood. On the windshield, a long crack spidered out from the bottom corner. Henry got out of the car and took a few steps into the driveway.

The sunlight definitely helped. Henry breathed deeply. Just being at the house of a dead man felt weird enough, but seeing the car made everything worse. It made it seem as if someone still lived there.

"What now?" Henry asked.

Kelvin stood beside the dead man's car, tracing the dents with a finger. When he finished, he motioned to Henry, and they circled the house in a large, slow loop, examining it from each side. The back featured large gardens and tall wooden lattices covered in ivy. The far side had cracked windows, which looked out from an elaborate dining room. At the front, a thick oak door sat beneath a magnificent gable flanked by gardens of flattened lilies and daisies.

At length, Henry and Kelvin stood back at the car shelter. "Now let's review the events on the night of the storm," Kelvin said. "Between the clerk and the newspaper, I think we have a pretty good idea of the going story."

Henry nodded. Kelvin produced a small notepad from a breast pocket and flipped to a page near the middle.

"All right, so we're home," Kelvin said. "It's

three days ago, June twentieth, at roughly nine fifteen p.m. We've finally gotten back after a long day of work at the bank. Right?"

"Right."

"Unfortunately, the car got pretty banged up on the drive, so we'll have to phone the insurance people later, but for now it's safe here under the shelter. And we're safe too, as long as we stay beside it. Hail is crashing down outside. Now what?"

Henry peered around the front of the house. He had only seen hail once before, when he and his parents took a trip to the Grand Canyon. A massive thunderstorm sprang up and stranded them for hours at the Vegas airport. Henry remembered sitting at the big airport windows with his parents, watching the falling ice smash against the tarmac. He tried to imagine that hail now, bouncing off Ed Wrightly's lawn. If they could get just under the roof at the front door, they'd be safe. He grabbed Kelvin's arm and they both stepped back into the safety of the car shelter.

"The door is pretty far away," Henry said. "We could run, but I wouldn't want to chance it. Can't we just stay here? Wait out the storm?"

Kelvin threw his hands up. "What, and be here all night? I have things to do, Henry! Besides…" And here he pointed a long index finger to the back corner of the shelter. "Why don't we just use a different door?" There, in the shadows, a small door led into the side of the house.

Henry winced. How'd he miss that? He walked up to it and peered through a dirty window. Furniture, unopened boxes, and junk of all sorts cluttered a dark room.

"It's a storage room, I think."

Kelvin knelt down and inspected the doorknob, dusting it with powder from a small bag in his pocket. "Hmm, nothing usable. Go ahead, give it a try."

Henry tried the door. "Locked." He cupped his eyes with his hands and looked inside again. Below the window sat a sturdy dresser, flush against the door. The door, he noticed, opened inward. "That's weird. The door is blocked. I don't think we could get in even with the key."

Kelvin rooted through his car and emerged with a flashlight. It cast a stark light onto the boxes and furniture. "You're right. Bad design." He lowered the flashlight. "Well, Wrightly couldn't get in that way, so neither can we. And since we don't want to be stuck here for hours, it's around to the front, right Henry?"

Henry looked into the front yard again, imagining the hail still beating down, bouncing off the now-flattened grass. "I guess. The umbrella should keep us safe, right?" He mimed opening an umbrella.

The reply sounded less than optimistic. "Well,

hail can be quite destructive. Farmers hate it because it destroys whole fields of crops."

"So…"

"So, no."

"Then we're running, huh?"

"Probably. On the count of three, we'll make a run for it." Kelvin leaned forward in a running stance.

Henry imagined the umbrella in his hand and pictured hail streaking down under the night sky ahead. Lightning crashed in the distance, illuminating the falling ice. It wouldn't feel good.

"One…" his uncle counted. "Two…"

Henry leaned forward.

"Three."

Henry pushed off the pavement hard, propelling himself forward into the storm. He made a curve toward the front door. The grassy yard stretched much farther than he would have liked, and the dark, cracking sky remained above him for several seconds too long. He braced against the sting of the hailstones. Any second now he could stumble, or slip on the wet grass, and then what? More bruises. Or worse. He pictured himself lying in the grass, struggling to stand.

Henry lunged up the steps to the front door, grabbing one of the columns to stop himself. He'd made it, safe under the roof! Now he would just get his keys, maybe light a fire tonight to dry off, have a glass of milk, and…

Wait, where was Kelvin?

Henry turned and saw his uncle standing out in the open, back near the car shelter, laughing. "I'm not actually going to run, Henry."

Henry flushed hotly.

"But thanks, that's just what we needed. It gives me a measure of where the dead man might have run. He was an older man and much fatter than yourself, of course, but I can make the necessary adjustments."

Saying this, Kelvin proceeded toward the door, hands clasped behind his back, scanning the ground near the path Henry had taken. He stopped a few times, picked at the grass, and then continued.

"Wrightly died 'not ten feet from his front door,' correct?" Kelvin asked, not looking up.

"Yeah. Think the storm left us anything?"

Kelvin didn't answer. He squatted down, narrowing his eyes at one particular spot in the long, flattened grass. He glanced up at the open sky, and then back at the ground. "Yes, right about here."

Henry stepped forward. Nothing looked unusual about the spot. Even so, he shuddered. He imagined what things must have looked like here three evenings ago, with lightning slashing through the gusty, swirling clouds overhead and hailstones crashing down to the earth in sheets. Down on the beach, the wind would have formed the ocean into huge swells that smashed onto the sand with white, hissing spray. And there, crumpled on the path before him, lay the unmoving body of the banker.

Kelvin reached out a hand. From under several blades of grass, squashed into the dirt and nearly hidden from view, he pulled a small scrap of black fabric. It looked smooth, but not delicate like silk.

Henry leaned forward. "What is it?"

Kelvin didn't take his eyes off it. "It's from an umbrella, I think."

"Mr. Wrightly's?"

A slight pause. "Maybe."

Henry didn't know what to make of it. It couldn't have been there long. It looked dirty, but new.

In the distance, Henry noticed something else. At the other end of the long yard that descended from the dead man's front steps, a group of six people marched closer.

"Kelvin." Henry gave his uncle a light rap on the shoulder. "You'll want to see this."

Chapter Six

Cooks, Salmons, and Rosenblooms

At about twenty paces away, the group stopped. Despite the low sun at their backs, Henry made out three men and three women. One of the men, a stout, bearded guy at the front, spoke up first. "What are you doing here?" His tone was rough, like a boxer ready to fight.

Henry wanted to take a step back. Kelvin took a step forward. "Let me introduce myself," he said in his sunny tone. "I'm Kelvin McCloud. This is my nephew, Henry." Kelvin held out his hand, but the man just eyed Kelvin, fists clenched. A slender, attractive woman stood by his side. The rest of the group remained silent, so Kelvin continued. "I'm a weather detective. I came here to investigate a storm."

Murmurs passed through the group. "A detective?"

"A private eye." Kelvin's hand disappeared

into his pocket. The man in front tensed visibly but relaxed when Kelvin pulled out an I.D. Kelvin handed it to the slender woman. After studying it, she let out a long breath.

"Absolutely nothing to worry about, Frank. You get into such a tizzy all the time, but it's just a man doing his job."

Each member of the group passed over the I.D. in turn, but the air of suspicion didn't ease. Henry noticed that one person in the group, a tall, athletic man in shorts and a striped polo shirt, gripped a baseball bat in a powerful hand. Round, painful-looking bruises ran down his arms and legs.

"I was under the impression the police had left," said the slender woman in a smooth, but not altogether friendly, tone.

"I'm not with the local police, ma'am."

In the back, the third man whispered something Henry couldn't hear to the bathrobe-clad woman beside him.

Kelvin took his I.D. back. "All of you were Mr. Wrightly's neighbors?"

"That's right." The bearded man's voice had lost only a touch of its earlier growl. "Frank Rosenbloom's the name. This is my wife, Josephina." He motioned to the slender woman, who smiled politely.

Henry couldn't help staring. Josephina Rosenbloom—she was the one quoted in the newspaper article. She and her husband looked like total opposites. Frank looked rough, stood only five feet tall, and possessed a long, pointed beard that ran down to the collar of his shirt. Josephina, standing beside him, possessed everything he lacked: height, grace, and confidence. Oversized sunglasses sat on her nose despite the dimming light, and a red pleated dress swished around her legs in the breeze, giving the impression that she had just walked out of the pages of a fashion magazine.

Talking in low voices, the other four people on the lawn looked suspicious and unhappy, but Frank pointed to each one in turn. "This is Elena and Rodger Salmon," he said, indicating the athletic man with the round bruises and a severe-looking woman dressed completely in deep purple beside him.

"Hi," said Rodger Salmon, but not a word more.

Elena Salmon said nothing. She leaned away from her husband with crossed arms and didn't so much as look in Henry and Kelvin's direction. Henry bit his tongue. Her puckered lips gave her face a fish-like quality. At any moment he expected Mrs. Salmon to flop wildly toward to the ocean and dive in.

"And I, sir, am Eugene Cook," said the man in the back in an easy southern drawl. Unlike the first four, in their breezy summer garb, he wore long seersucker clothing and a tan hat. "This here's my wife Isabel." To his side, Isabel Cook smiled politely. Despite the gesture, she looked tired and cold, clutching a well-worn blue-green bathrobe around herself. "Told her to stay in bed, but she'd have none of it."

"One can't be in bed all day," Isabel replied in a tone more melodious than her husband's. "Mr. McCloud, you mentioned—" A loud and nasal fit of coughing interrupted her sentence. "You mentioned you are a weather detective. May I ask what that is?"

"Yeah," Rodger Salmon agreed forcefully. "Just what do you do?"

Kelvin smiled politely. "A weather detective," he responded with a slight bow, "is someone who detects by using the weather."

The six neighbors on the lawn stared at Kelvin, baffled. A tinge of bafflement struck Henry as well. His uncle had never bowed to anyone before. It must be another act.

"Since the earth and ocean and atmosphere are all part of one big complex system," Kelvin went on, "knowing about the weather can help me unravel certain types of mysteries. I am here," he concluded, "to look into the storm that killed Edward Wrightly."

Eugene Cook furrowed his eyebrows. "I must admit, sir, I don't properly understand. You know about weather?"

Josephina
+ Frank
Rosenbloom

"I do indeed."

"And the atmosphere?" asked Josephina Rosenbloom, peering over her sunglasses.

"Of course. And science to boot."

Rodger Salmon, the athletic man with the baseball bat, spoke up next. "So, like..." He looked around himself. Behind him, the sun hung low, spreading shades of red and yellow above the row of houses on the far side of the distant street. "So if you're a weather detective, why's the sunset red?"

Henry hid a grin. They were testing his uncle. Boy, would they be surprised.

"Ah, a fine question!" replied Kelvin. He sounded slightly loopy, and Henry needed no more convincing that this was an act.

Kelvin pointed westward. "The answer starts with the sun. Sunlight travels across ninety-three million miles of space to reach where you and I are standing right now. It's a long journey, I know, but most of those eight minutes are pretty uneventful. When sunlight hits the atmosphere, however, something incredible happens. While most of the light goes straight through, some of the blue light— white light is made of all the colors of the rainbow, you know—collides with gas molecules in the air. Do you know what gases are most common in the air?"

Rodger paused, stunned. "Uh," he stammered, "uh... oxygen?"

"That's one," replied Kelvin, playing the schoolteacher. "We need that to breathe."

"And there's nitrogen," replied Josephina excitedly. "It's the most common."

Kelvin gave a small jump. "Exactly right! And when light hits those nitrogen and oxygen molecules, some of the blue gets scattered around. It bounces all through the air, making the sky blue during the day. The yellow and red light comes more or less straight at us, giving the sun some of its yellowish color. Red and yellow light only start to scatter when they have to pass through a lot of air. And when does that happen?"

Kelvin looked at them expectantly, waiting for a reply. As the people on the lawn thought, Henry admired his uncle's act. By playing the harmless, eccentric professor, Kelvin could disarm their suspicions. Kelvin *was* eccentric, of course, but hardly harmless.

Still, Henry thought about his uncle's question too. Being diligent in thinking through questions was something that Kelvin had stressed to him time and time again. It was a trait Kelvin shared with Henry's dad, Arthur Alabaster.

The spectacled eyes and gruff smile of Henry's father appeared in his memory. In Henry's younger years, his dad had given him many pieces of advice, but emphasized none of them more strongly than this: "Whenever you can, Henry, think through an idea yourself. This is vitally important. Ask others, definitely, but always remember to think. You'll be a better person for it."

These words faded away to Eugene Cook's confident reply. "I say, that happens at morning and evening, of course. That's when light has to go longways through the atmosphere to get here."

Kelvin gave a single loud, excited clap of his hands. "Couldn't have said it better myself! So right now, even though people in California are seeing blue, and people in Europe are seeing stars, we're getting the reds and yellows, which fill the sky beautifully. Pollution can make a sunset redder, but it's the air molecules which do most of the work."

Hands on his sides, Kelvin turned to look out at the sunset. The sun now hung just above the houses on the far side of the road. "Beautiful," he said with a sigh that struck Henry as a bit over the top. "Are those your houses?"

Rodger Salmon pointed to a pinkish-orange one. "Well, that one is Elena's and mine."

"But yes, all of us live on that side of the street," said Josephina Rosenbloom. "We can't afford to live on this side, tragically. Oceanfront property is very expensive, you know."

Henry decided it was time he spoke up. "So why'd you all come up here tonight?" He nodded toward the baseball bat still clutched in Rodger Salmon's hand.

Rodger Salmon stammered, and Frank Rosenbloom laughed. It was a relief to find that Kelvin's ploy had worked. The neighbors all seemed much more at ease. If any of these people really did have anything to hide, they probably wouldn't worry too much about the investigation of some youngster and his oblivious uncle.

"Actually," Frank replied, "we thought you were those rascal kids again."

"Kids?"

Josephina nodded matter-of-factly. "A group of teenagers, dear. They've been up here both nights since the storm that killed Ed, doing God knows what. We haven't gotten a good look at them, but it's horrible. We found beer cans both mornings."

Eugene Cook rubbed his arm through a paint-covered sleeve and grimaced. "I say, is that what y'all are here for? To look into that nuisance?"

Kelvin shook his head. "Afraid not. Just the weather."

"Were the teenagers up here in the storm?" Henry asked.

The Rosenblooms, Salmons, and Cooks all looked at each other, but nobody came up with a decent answer. "Not that any of us saw."

Kelvin stared at the sky. He wasn't taking any notes, Henry noticed, nor did he seem to be paying much attention at all. Henry took out a pad of his own and wrote *Teenagers?*

"It was probably a lovely storm that night," Kelvin said. "Were you all here to see it?"

One by one, all six neighbors described what they saw and where they were that night.

Frank and Josephina Rosenbloom both stayed home. The hail came down in torrents, and thunder cracked like breaking boulders. They saw one car pull into Edward Wrightly's driveway that evening, at maybe quarter after nine.

Eugene Cook attended a movie in town, so he missed most of the squall, but watched the end of it from outside the theater after the power went out.

Isabel Cook participated in a book club in the neighborhood (she said through sniffles). They discussed *Dracula* and tried to ignore the monstrous storm.

Rodger Salmon lounged at a bar in town, The Mariner's Draught, and drank as the streets outside flooded.

Elena Salmon didn't answer. She looked away in tight-lipped silence. Rodger answered for her. She also attended the book club, and then went home.

Kelvin nodded repeatedly. "Well, sounds like quite a storm."

"Did any of you drive in it?" Henry asked, picturing Mr. Wrightly's pock-marked sedan.

The neighbors shook their heads. They had each left their cars in safe places and just waited out the storm.

Henry jotted this down. He and Kelvin now had only one question left. Leading the group into the car shelter, Henry pointed at the small door leading into the side of the manor.

"Did Mr. Wrightly never use that door? I mean, I think it's blocked."

Eugene Cook laughed, answering in his thick southern drawl. "That there was one of the old boy's oddities. Ed he could be a right strange fellow, and he just never liked that door. If he was going to live in a place like this, he said, with the big entrance and spires and gardens and all, well, whatever else, you'd never find him entering through the garage like a raccoon. He was to do it in fashion, through the front. Those were his words, mind you. If it's blocked, he probably did it on purpose."

Henry had a hard time believing this, but the other neighbors nodded in agreement.

"Yup," said Rodger. "Hated it. Said the contractor wouldn't let him build the place without it."

The group now started to look weary of questions, so Kelvin pulled a few cards from his pocket, jotted his room number on the corners, and handed them out. "Well, thank you all very much. If you recall anything else about the storm, or any other weird things from that night, please call or stop by. We'll be here a few days more, enjoying the sights."

The three couples each took a card and, with the Rosenblooms and the Cooks chatting and the

Salmons in awkward silence, they departed down the gentle slope toward their houses. Henry watched the small figures recede. Once they were out of earshot, he handed Kelvin his notepad, now full of notes. "What do you think?" The look of happy ignorance slid from Kelvin's features. "There's something interesting about each of them, undoubtedly. For instance, how did Rodger Salmon get hailstone bruises? Why is Elena Salmon so angry? When did Isabel Cook get her cold? It is details like these that often yield the most interesting answers." Kelvin paged through Henry's notes. "Let's be careful not to get ahead of ourselves, though. We still don't even know if a crime has been committed."

Henry nodded. Behind them, the dark spires of the manor reached toward the evening sky. "Well, want to look inside? I bet we could get one of those broken windows open."

Returning the notepad, Kelvin stretched his arms. He stared out at the last rays of the sun, setting in the distance beyond Rodger Salmon's pink-orange house. "No, that's enough for tonight. We should get some dinner."

Henry stepped up beside his uncle. The last bit of the sun slipped below the horizon, leaving only the red and yellow painted sky. The earth continued its slow spin, placing Henry and Kelvin at the edge of the planet's shadow.

Eugene + Isabel Cook

Henry's stomach gurgled. Kelvin was right. They'd found out enough for today. Whatever was coming next, it could wait.

Chapter Seven

The Hotel at Night

Henry lay awake in his stiff bed, staring through darkness. On the far bed, near the humming AC, his uncle snored.

How could Kelvin sleep on a night like this? Electricity pulsed through Henry's veins as he pondered the day's discoveries: the hotel clerk's story, the black umbrella scrap in the grass, the jumpy neighbors, the suspicious teenagers at night. Everything he and Kelvin had learned just hinted at larger unknowns.

Henry thought back to the woman in the yellow dress. He imagined that long blond hair again, vanishing into the stairwell. Had that really happened just last night? Henry turned on his side and closed his eyes. The snake in his belly coiled tighter. Who was that woman? Why did she run? Soon these thoughts started to fade.

Thump. Henry woke. Had he heard something? The clock on the nightstand read eleven forty-three p.m. Half an hour had passed. Kelvin still snored lightly on the nearby bed.

The sound came again, a muffled thump against the closed door. Next came silence, then soft footsteps, getting softer.

The woman in the yellow dress! Henry slipped from bed. Grabbing a keycard from the nightstand, he slunk to the hallway door. No letter lay on the floor this time. He gripped the steel handle and swung the door open.

He leaned forward. An empty hallway stretched away to the left.

To the right, a shadow disappeared around a corner.

Should he wake Kelvin? No time. He slunk down the blue and brown paisley hallway, his heart jolting up and down in his chest.

What if this wasn't the woman from New York, but someone worse?

At the corner, Henry flattened himself against the wall, taking three deep breaths before peering around it. Halfway down that hallway, a stairwell door swung shut.

Henry dashed from the corner. She wouldn't escape him this time. He slipped through the door and followed.

Sounds of movement came from farther down.

56

"Hey!"

The word leapt from Henry's mouth before he could stop himself. It echoed loudly in the enclosed stairwell, but the sounds of movement continued. No stopping now. Henry jumped down the stairs two at a time.

"Hey, stop!" he yelled again.

And, surprisingly, the figure did stop.

It caught Henry off guard. Rounding a turn in a wild run, he missed his footing and stumbled. He careened right toward the figure, who was not, after all, the woman from New York. It was a young black girl.

For a second, everything became tumbling commotion. Something, which might have been an elbow, struck Henry in the chest. A wall came toward him with alarming speed. Or was that the floor? It met him with a crack.

"Ow!" The girl untangled herself from Henry. "What's your problem?" She kicked out at Henry and he scuttled away.

"Sorry," he said. The girl stared at him. Before she could say anything else, he blurted, "Did you see a woman?"

Surprise and confusion replaced anger in the girl's eyes. "A woman?"

"Yeah, I must have just missed her. Uh, tall, with blond hair about this long." He motioned with his hand.

The girl stood up. "No. Everyone's in bed. Are you crazy or something?"

Henry gave her a desperate look. Silence hung thick in the stairwell. He jumped to his feet, ready to search the hotel top to bottom until he found the woman. Then the obvious truth smacked him in the face like a shovel.

"Then was it you? At my door, on the third floor? Room 327?"

The girl shrugged. "Maybe. Could've been." The light blue scrunchie around her ponytail matched her light blue pajamas. Henry had seen her before. The girl from the lobby. "Did it sound like this?" Making her hand into a fist, she thumped the stairwell door.

Henry just stared at her. She narrowed her eyes. "What's the big deal, anyway? I just bumped the door. Didn't think anyone would even notice."

"I, uh…" Henry couldn't find his words. "I thought you were someone else."

"Someone to chase? In the middle of the night? Boy, that is strange." For the first time, she grinned at him.

Henry rubbed a hand through his messy hair. Should he be offended? The adrenaline was wearing off. "Well, what about you? You're bumping on people's doors you don't even know."

The girl stretched her arms, turning away. "I wasn't tired." Her answer echoed slightly in the stairwell. "Mom and Pop can be so boring sometimes. They went to bed, but I wanted something to do." She opened the stairwell door and started to step out into a hallway. "Coincidentally, did you know I couldn't find a single ghost in this place? Not one!"

For a moment Henry hesitated. Ghosts? The woman in the yellow dress sprang into his mind, making him shiver.

The girl stared at him. "Well, come on, slowpoke."

Henry grabbed the door and followed. They emerged into a wide blue hallway on the first floor, somewhere deep in one of the many wings of the hotel. The color of the walls made Henry feel as if they were underwater. "Where are you going, anyway?"

The girl didn't look back. "I told you already. I'm trying to find something to do, duh. This place is so dull. Doesn't look it, but it is." She ran her fingers along the wall.

"Don't your parents mind that you're out?"

She shrugged. "Probably not. They're so busy with work. I could run away and they wouldn't notice for a day."

Henry didn't know what to say, so he nodded. He'd never thought about running away from his own parents. Even Kelvin, the aloof uncle, would freak out if he disappeared for a whole day. Still, something about the girl's demeanor appealed to him. She seemed like the type of person who wouldn't hesitate to wrestle with an alligator. She'd just put on a pair of waterproof boots, clap her hands together, and jump right in.

Right in character she held out a hand. "So anyway, my name's Rachel."

Her palm felt soft and friendly, and Henry said, "All right, Rachel. I'm Henry. Sorry about running into you."

She probed her shoulder with a finger, and then shrugged. "It's okay. Just don't do it again, capeesh?"

Ahead, the hall diverged, with corridors splitting off to the left and right at forty-five degree angles. Both ways looked identical, but Rachel, with only a second of decision-making, chose a direction and kept going.

"So why are you here?" Henry asked. "In Sandy Run, I mean."

"Vacation." Rachel rolled her eyes. "Supposedly. But Mom and Pop haven't stopped working yet. They're both accountants, so all day long it's money this and profits that, just on and on and on. We've been here three days and I haven't been to the beach yet!" She scuffed the floor with her foot. "What about you?"

Henry's chest swelled. "A murder. Well, no, not a murder, I guess. At least maybe not. My uncle's a detective. We came to check out some guy who died in a thunderstorm."

Rachel's eyes grew huge. "Oh cool, I heard about

that. We were here when it happened. Pretty wild storm. But wasn't it an accident?"

"Maybe. It's hard to tell. Some woman slipped us a note and some money last night. That's what got us started." Henry paused, wondering if he should be talking about all of this to someone he didn't really know. What would Kelvin say?

Still, Rachel looked honest enough. The freckles on her face stood out when she smiled. "That's totally cool! It's just you and your uncle?"

"Yeah."

"Not your parents?"

"They're not really around anymore."

Rachel froze. "Oh man, sorry."

Henry shook his head. "No, it's okay."

"So they're dead?" Rachel clasped a hand over her mouth, her eyes wide.

Henry answered anyway. "I'm really not sure. Nobody's certain what happened."

"They might be okay?"

Henry shrugged. An awful pain boiled up in his chest, but he didn't want to show it. "I don't think so. They were in a little plane somewhere near England when it happened. Just them and a couple others, heading to a physics conference. That's when they got into the storm. I don't really know what happened. The news said the plane must have gone down over the Atlantic, but nobody ever found it."

Henry didn't tell the rest of the story. He didn't tell how, for months afterward, he kept thinking his parents were okay and would return soon, and how one morning he would wake up to the smell of waffles and bacon and find his parents downstairs cooking breakfast and laughing. To tell the truth, he was still waiting for that.

"That happened last fall," he said. "I've been living with Uncle Kelvin ever since."

Rachel bit her lip. An awkward silence lingered between them. They reached the end of a long hallway and stood at a pair of glass doors. Outside, concrete walkways surrounded a dark rectangular pool. In the black sky above, Henry couldn't see any stars at all.

"I'm sorry," Rachel said quietly.

Henry shook his head. The constricted, serpentine feeling coiled in his stomach, but it gradually lessened. "Whatever. It's not your fault." Henry pressed his hand to the glass. "You think we can go out?"

Rachel blinked. "Beats me." They both reached for the lever at the same moment, but a lock kept the door shut.

Henry sighed, stepping back. "Any cool rooms to find around here?"

"You'd think so, but *nada*. I always wonder what kind of people stay in these weird places."

"That's why you bumped our door?"

"Exactly, but I'm always too chicken to stick around."

Henry smiled. He was glad she had woken him up.

For another hour or so, Henry and Rachel peeked down twisting hallways and into dark common rooms, talking about life and looking for ghosts. Rachel wanted to do this, and Henry just went along with her at first, but he soon found the fun in it. Rachel took a pad from her pocket and showed him sketches of what some specters might look like. Some of the details were pretty gruesome. Henry searched near the vending machines and Rachel put her ear against the wall and closed her eyes, listening.

At well past one-thirty, Rachel stomped her foot. "Not one ghost here! You'd think this old place would be full of dead people."

"Yeah, too bad." Henry let out a long, sleepy yawn. "Maybe we should get back to bed."

"Maybe. Nice meeting you, Henry."

At the lobby, they started up the blue stairs. Somewhere below them, a telephone rang. "Sandy Run Inn," a woman answered politely. "How may I help you?"

"Hey," Rachel chirped, ignoring the phone conversation, "you'll be here a couple days, right?"

Henry nodded.

"Want to do something tomorrow? My parents

will be working again, but I bet we could have some fun."

"Sure." In the background, the young woman continued to talk.

"Cool," Rachel said. "We're in room 215."

"My uncle and I are in 327."

Rachel gave an embarrassed smile. "I know."

Henry laughed. The clerk's happy chatter continued in the distance below. Her words echoed up to them. "Oh yes, your friend is staying here. Checked in just this afternoon…" Henry and Rachel continued up the stairwell. "Ah, here it is. He's in room 327."

Henry nearly missed a step. Did she say room 327? That's where he and Kelvin were staying, but they hadn't told anyone back home. The dead man's neighbors were the only ones who knew, and they'd been told to call the cell.

A few steps farther up, Rachel stopped too. "What's up?"

Henry didn't respond. He took one tentative step back down the stairs. More words from the conversation drifted up to him. "That's right, room 327. We have them down for, let's see…three nights."

Henry's eyes grew wide. He had heard right. Room 327. Their room! He tried to rationalize it, reassure himself, but he couldn't. Nobody should be calling for them.

Below, Henry heard the clerk conclude. "You're

very... oh, hello?" The sound of the receiver clicking broke Henry from his daze. He ran back down the stairs, shooting right for the front counter.

Henry grabbed the edge of the counter and stopped. "Oh!" the young woman said with a jump. "Why, hello."

"Who was that?"

"What?" The look of surprise didn't fade from the woman's face, but now a tinge of confusion landed there as well.

"That person, just now, on the phone," Henry said. "Who was it?"

The woman paused. She readjusted herself on her stool and that pleasant, professional look service people sometimes wear returned to her face.

"Young man, don't you think it's a little late for—"

Henry didn't let her finish. "Listen," he said, "this is important. I need to know who you were talking to."

The woman paused a second time. The professional look gave way to the dumbfounded one again. "Important?"

Rachel arrived at Henry's side. He nodded rapidly. "My uncle and I are the ones in 327. Kelvin McCloud—that's who the person asked for, right?"

"Well, yes, but—"

"So who was it?"

The woman put a hand to her cheek, leaning

forward. "Well I'm sorry, young man, but I can't say. Hotel rules."

Rachel glared at the woman. "But you could give out Henry's room number, huh? Hotels aren't supposed to do that, you know."

The clerk opened and shut her mouth, but nothing came out.

"So who was it?" Rachel said.

"Well, I... She didn't give a name."

Henry's heart leapt. "It was a woman? How old did she sound? In her forties?"

"Possibly. I didn't get her name. She hung up afterward."

Henry glanced at Rachel, a smile breaking out across his lips. Rachel looked back in confusion.

The woman tapped the counter with a fingernail. "But what are you two doing up anyway? It's a quarter till two." She made a shooing motion with her hands as if they were small pests. "There's nothing more I can say. Get to bed."

Henry stared at her, but he knew he wouldn't get any more answers. Without another word, he and Rachel ran up the stairs. As soon as they were out of earshot, Rachel turned on him sharply.

"What in the world was that about?"

"It's her!" Henry said. His stomach twisted and turned like a snake. "It's her. The woman from New York, the one who left us the note. She's followed us here."

Chapter Eight

The Light in the Yard

The next morning came too soon, and too brightly. Already up and dressed, Kelvin stood in the light from the window, straightening his blue, cloud-patterned tie. "Going to the police station today," he said. "Then the bank. Won't be gone long. You can sleep."

Henry pulled the covers up over his head. The door clicked shut. A while later, after a groggy breakfast, he headed down to Rachel's room.

On the way, he thought about last night. After their encounter with the night clerk, Henry and Rachel sat in the blue-carpeted stairwell for another hour or more, quickly and quietly discussing the mysterious woman from New York. They both felt as if they had fallen into some dark and dangerous plot, and they jumped every time someone appeared below them on the steps. But every time, it was just some tired looking man or woman, shambling off to bed.

Henry arrived at room 215. Rachel's room. He knocked. The door opened and a tall woman waved him in. "Come in, come in." Halfway through the second 'come in', she had already buzzed back to her desk. "You must be the boy from upstairs. Harold, was it?"

"Henry," said Henry.

"Oh of course, come in!"

That was three times now. Rachel emerged from the bathroom. She slouched against the wall in shorts and a yellow T-shirt, yawning.

"Hi, Henry. These are my parents, Vanessa and Clarence."

Seated at a second desk in the far corner of the room, a round-faced man looked up from behind several tall stacks of paper and waved. "Clarence Willowby. Nice to meet you, Harold."

Henry waved back. "Uh, nice to meet you, too."

Clarence Willowby returned to his paperwork, nearly disappearing behind the towers of paper. "So what are you two doing today? Your mom and I have to finish up the Jones account, Rachel, so I'm afraid we can't take you to the beach like we thought."

Rachel gave a half-hearted smile. "Yeah. Just going outside for a bit. That okay?"

Vanessa smiled, buzzing over to a set of binders stacked on the dresser. "Yes, that sounds fine, doesn't it, Clarence?" Clarence nodded distractedly, already consumed in his work. "I hear Sandy Run is a very safe town," she said. "Just don't go far. And mind the roads."

"Sure." Rachel pushed Henry into the hall. "We'll be safe. Love you." She shut the door.

"So what are we doing?" Henry asked.

"Anything's better than staying here. Come on." A minute later, the sun glared down on them through a clear blue sky, and the large glass hotel doors chimed shut behind.

Henry and Rachel spent most of the morning exploring bits of Sandy Run. The tree-lined streets near the hotel looked lively and interesting enough and, as Vanessa said, they seemed safe. Down one alley Henry and Rachel found a magic shop, where they marveled at paper that could disappear in a puff of fire and tall hats with false bottoms. Down another alley was an ice cream parlor, where they gorged on scoops of chocolate frozen yogurt and strawberry sorbet.

Passing a third street, Henry spotted two people he recognized. It took him a minute to remember. It was Rodger and Elena Salmon, the athletic man and his puckering wife.

"Hold up." He motioned for Rachel to stop. They retreated a few steps to the corner.

"I still just can't believe it, Rodger," Elena said, spitting out the words in a low hiss. "I trusted you,

Elena + Rodger Salmon

and now we're worse off than ever. How could you do it?"

"I don't know..." he sputtered, motioning with his hands. "I just..."

"Did you even think about the consequences? How long have you been sneaking off to that bank anyway? Now we'll have to—"

The words died on her lips. Elena glared at Henry and Rachel with a bitter, stony-faced scowl. Without another word, she hurried her husband the opposite way down the narrow cobblestone alley.

Rachel's eyes widened. "What was that all about?"

Henry shook his head. The couple vanished from sight, no doubt hustling away down the winding streets of the town. Henry considered following, but all he could think of was Edward Wrightly, lying dead in the grass, not ten feet from his front door.

"Well Henry, I'm—" Coming through the hotel room door, Kelvin stopped, mid-stride. "Oh, hello. And who is this?"

Henry glanced up. He and Rachel sat on the carpet in the center of the room, surrounded by notes and drawings of everything that happened in Sandy Run so far. They'd spent the last hour making them, with Henry writing the notes and describing what he'd seen to Rachel, and Rachel drawing out illustrations and diagrams.

Henry straightened himself up. "Hi, Kelvin. This is Rachel Willowby."

Rachel pushed aside a drawing of Rodger and Elena arguing in the alleyway. "Hey. My folks are staying downstairs."

"Ah." Kelvin finished stepping into the room and put down his briefcase. "Well, it's nice to meet you, Rachel."

"Yup, you too, Dr. McCloud."

A frown creased Kelvin's face. "Mr. McCloud will do just fine, thank you."

Rachel looked at Henry, who shrugged. This was something he'd never figured out about his uncle. Ever since losing his professor position at Stuyvesant, his old university, Kelvin had returned to using Mister rather than Doctor. Perhaps Kelvin thought it would put people more at ease. But Henry suspected the reasons ran deeper. Kelvin had always been very proud of his old job, and Henry sensed a great deal of regret in his uncle concerning the ordeal that had followed.

Henry let the point pass. Gathering some of the drawings, he and Rachel stood. They told Kelvin about the squabble between Elena and Rodger Salmon in the alleyway.

Kelvin glanced at the pictures and notes. "Hmm…" After a few seconds, he raised his long eyebrows and looked straight at Henry. "So I take it Rachel here is our new consultant for this investigation?"

Henry felt his face grow warm. He opened his mouth, stammering for something to say.

Kelvin smiled. "It's all right. I suppose we can let one person in on our investigation. And you can tell your parents about it too, Rachel, but nobody else, okay? I don't want anyone in Sandy Run to know we're potentially looking for a murderer. This whole investigation will go much more smoothly if we can get people to lower their guards."

"Sure, I can keep it on the DL," Rachel said with a nod.

"Good. So Henry told you what we do?"

"You're a weather detective. Sounds cool."

Kelvin tried to conceal a smile, but failed. He sat down on the bed and paged through Rachel's drawings. "Okay, knowing about this argument helps us. Rodger Salmon did something he shouldn't have, and I suspect it may have happened on the night of the murder. You saw those hailstone bruises on him, right Henry? Anyone caught out in the hailstorm would have gotten some of those. He told us he stayed at a bar that night, but maybe he went somewhere else. Maybe he went to the bank. Good work, you two."

Remembering their other escapade, Henry told Kelvin about overhearing the woman from New York last night.

"You were up last night? When?"

Henry fidgeted awkwardly. "Late. You'd gone to bed."

They discussed the encounter for several minutes, but came to no conclusions.

"What about the police station?" Rachel asked. "Henry told me you went there. Learn anything?"

The corners of Kelvin's mouth flicked downward. He reclined on the bed. "Not too much. The cause of death was definitely the blow to the back of his... oh." Kelvin dropped the sentence. His sharp gray eyes stared at Rachel. "But you probably don't..."

Rachel smiled. "Go on. I'm no lightweight."

Kelvin gave a hearty laugh. "Ah, very good. It's always nice to have a little boldness in your life. Keeps things interesting. But yes, Wrightly died from being struck in the head. The police permitted me to visit the morgue to see, but it was difficult to make any conclusions beyond that. The body was covered with hailstone welts." Kelvin paused, his mouth still slightly open. He closed it and swallowed. "Actually, I'm afraid I didn't make a very good showing of myself there. I don't imagine the police like having to clean up people's breakfasts. Still, they could tell me two things for certain: that Edward Wrightly was out in the storm that night, and that's where he died, in his yard."

"They still say it was the hail?" Henry asked.

Kelvin nodded. "But they may have missed something. That's what we're here to find out."

Rachel sat down at a small table opposite the bed. She leaned forward on her elbows. "How about the bank? You went there too, right?"

Kelvin slumped back farther on the bed. He spoke at the ceiling. "Yes, I went there. The other employees said Wrightly was a workaholic. Some people liked him, others didn't. Standard stuff. They said he built that huge manor of his about a year and a half ago. Wouldn't stop talking about it for months. Things like that definitely could have raised some ire among his coworkers."

Kelvin paused, narrowing his eyes.

"I met another of Wrightly's neighbors at the bank. Mrs. Victoria Sharp. She worked there under Wrightly, and she seemed very cold about his death. Here's the strange part, though. Remember those teenagers we were told about, who were up at the manor on the nights after the storm? Well, when I asked Victoria about them, she insisted that was a lie. She stayed quite clear on that point: there had been no teenagers."

Henry frowned. "Weird."

A loud knock resounded at the door. Henry jumped. All three fell silent.

"Are you two expecting anyone?" Kelvin mouthed.

Henry and Rachel both shook their heads. They watched as Kelvin stood and crept to the door. He put his eye to the peephole. A pause. Stepping back, he opened the door.

On the other side stood the portly, bearded Frank Rosenbloom.

"Ah, hello Mr. Rosenbloom," Kelvin said, slipping back into the over-expressive act from yesterday.

Henry let out a deep breath.

"You know this guy?" Rachel asked in Henry's ear.

"We met him yesterday. One of the dead man's neighbors."

"Mr. McCloud," said Frank Rosenbloom, looking excited but a bit awkward. "I wanted to talk to you about something."

Kelvin opened the door wider and stepped aside. "Come right in. What is it?"

Frank entered. His beard swayed from side to side as he walked to the nearer bed. "Well, you said we should tell you if we remembered anything about the storm. I had some time on my lunch break, so I..."

"Yes?"

"I came over. Josephina and I, we remember seeing something in Ed's yard that night." Frank tried sitting down, but looked equally awkward there. "We saw a light."

Henry echoed the words from his seat. "A light?"

Frank nodded. "Yup. It was pretty faint, and flickering. I thought my eyes were playing tricks on me, what with the hail coming down so hard, but Josephina said she saw it too, and she always sees the right things. It was coming from Ed's back yard, just out of sight behind the right side of the house, from our point of view."

"A flashlight?" Rachel offered. "Or lightning? It was definitely flashing quite a bit around here."

Pulling at his beard, Frank shrugged. "It sure beats me. If it was lightning, it's the weirdest I've ever seen. It happened just before the car pulled up Ed's driveway."

"Fascinating," Kelvin mused, a hand to his chin. "What time did you see this light?"

"Started at ten after nine, pretty much exactly. Josephina and I were in the middle of some TV."

"Anything good?" Henry asked. Frank Rosenbloom listed the shows. Pretending to draw, Henry jotted them down. He'd seen this trick in a movie one time. Later, he'd check the channel guide to see if Frank had lied.

"Notice anything else?" Kelvin asked.

Frank shook his head.

Kelvin shrugged. "Oh well. Still, it's intriguing. Thanks for letting me know." He shot his finger into the air, seeming to remember something. "Oh! One other thing. I went to the bank today. Don't know how we started talking about it, but Victoria Sharp told me she never saw any teenagers at Mr. Wrightly's place, on any of the nights since the death."

For the first time, Mr. Rosenbloom looked something other than awkward, bearded, and pudgy. He looked shocked. "What? But there were. I heard them up there myself, laughing and hollering at two a.m. And come to think of it, I know Victoria saw them. A light came on in her window at the same time on the second night."

"Which light?" Kelvin asked.

"Not sure. One of the bedrooms, I guess."

"How long was the light on?"

"Twenty seconds, maybe."

"What about the other neighbors?" Rachel asked. "Anyone else see this stuff?"

Kelvin cast a subtle, uneasy glance in Rachel's direction, but said nothing. Mr. Rosenbloom looked at her too, a dumbfounded expression creeping over his face. "I suppose not. I think Josephina and I were the only ones who heard the teenagers, but everyone saw the beer cans the next morning. I guess I told them the rest."

Henry leaned forward. "So what about Victoria? She sounded pretty sure."

Frank Rosenbloom sat up straighter, his cheeks starting to flush. "How would I know why Victoria told you that? She's an awful woman. I'll let you know she never liked Ed, or any of us. She'd say anything to make us look bad."

Kelvin smiled, raising his hands. "Well, it doesn't matter to me, anyway. Hmm, weird lightning.

Maybe there is something interesting in this case after all."

Henry nodded. "Good. That black fabric we found last time hasn't led anywhere."

Henry shut his mouth. He probably shouldn't have said that in front of their guest. Sitting on the bed, Frank Rosenbloom slowly raised his head. "Black fabric?"

Kelvin shot Henry a dirty look. "Oh, probably nothing. We just found a scrap of umbrella in the yard. Mr. Wrightly carried an umbrella, right? Must have been his. Hailstorms can break things pretty easily, you know. Did you know that falling hailstones can reach speeds of—"

Frank's eyes grew wide. "But Mr. McCloud," he said. "Stop. You have something wrong."

Kelvin stopped. In the quiet hotel room, Frank Rosenbloom went on.

"You said it was a piece of black fabric. Ed did have an umbrella that night. But it wasn't black. It was red."

Chapter Nine

The Black Mark

"Red!" Henry nearly jumped out of his seat. "How do you know that?"

Frank started. All eyes had turned to him. He stared back wide-eyed, looking like a dog who'd been caught tearing trash apart in the kitchen. "W-w-well," he sputtered, "all his friends knew it! A bright red umbrella with a heavy steel handle. I found it the next morning, blown right up to my house. It was tattered and blown inside out, with a big dent in the handle, but it was his."

"You're sure about that?" Kelvin insisted. "You couldn't be mistaken?"

"No. I knew it soon as I saw it. Red as an apple." The stout man paused. "Though some apples are green or yellow."

"Where's the umbrella now?" Henry asked.

"No idea. It disappeared. I figured the police

81

took it, but I can't say for sure." A look of worry passed like a cloud over Frank's features. "Wait, why's everyone staring at me? What's this mean?"

Kelvin immediately strode over to Frank. "Oh," he said with a laugh, helping the chubby man to his feet. "Nothing. Just wanted the umbrella for my weather museum, to show what hail can do. Henry mixed up the color, that's all. Well, look at the time. Your lunch break is probably over. Thank you very much. Goodbye, Mr. Rosenbloom."

Kelvin shut the door firmly. In the now quiet room, Henry and Rachel remained still, letting the implications of Mr. Rosenbloom's words sink in. Henry looked at Rachel, sitting with her chin on her fist. Rachel stared at Kelvin, standing with his back pressed against the door. Mr. Rosenbloom, now out in the hallway, could be heard muttering as he stalked off.

"Why, and all I was trying to do was…"

The words drifted away. Rachel finally spoke, her voice barely louder than a breath. "Someone else was with the dead guy that night."

"Someone," Henry added, "with a black umbrella."

"We don't know that for certain," Kelvin warned. "There could be any number of explanations. And as for the disappearance of Wrightly's umbrella, while it's suspicious, it isn't concrete evidence of anything."

Despite his uncle's words, Henry once again

imagined the scene at Ed Wrightly's towering mansion on the night of the storm—hail pelting down, lightning slashing through the sky, and the body of the banker lying in the battered grass.

But now some other person stood there—some dark figure beneath a black umbrella, standing over the body.

Kelvin removed himself from the door. Grabbing his pad, he jotted down some notes. Henry checked the TV listings—the shows Frank Rosenbloom had mentioned were all there. Rachel wondered aloud what they should do next. It would be best, they all agreed, to go back to the dead man's estate and find what they had missed. Kelvin pulled a long tan overcoat and a wide-brimmed hat from his luggage—his detective clothes, naturally—and, telling Rachel that she could come along provided she got her parents' permission, he got ready to leave.

Ten minutes later they all sat in the car, bumping toward the dead man's estate. In the back seat, Henry and Rachel discussed their four new questions.

First, what was the strange light Frank and Josephina saw in Ed Wrightly's back yard on the night of the murder?

Second, what ultimately happened to the dead man's umbrella, and why did it disappear?

Third, how could teenagers both have been at

the estate and not been there on the two nights following the murder? ("Schrödinger's kiddies," Kelvin joked from the front seat, cracking himself up.)

Fourth, why did a light come on in Victoria's house at two a.m. two nights after the death?

Henry and Rachel also discussed, darkly, who might have been in the yard with Edward Wrightly on the night he died. Kelvin warned them that their "second person idea" remained just a hypothesis, but struggled to explain when else a second umbrella might have gotten torn up recently.

"Even a hailstorm is a bit of a stretch," he said.

Ahead, the large estate came into view. Rumbling past the simple white mailbox, Kelvin turned up the long driveway. The black luxury sedan still sat at the far end, dented and abandoned.

Kelvin jolted them to a stop and all three stepped out. As before, the sound of crashing waves met Henry's ears. Beyond the supports of the car shelter, the ocean stretched away beneath a brighter sky than yesterday. A few seabirds squawked, making short, jumpy flights from one patch of ground to another. Rachel took a few steps toward the beach, staring at the horizon. Henry stood beside her, smelling the salty air.

"Come on, you two. We're here for a reason." Kelvin stood in the middle of the back yard, staring at them.

Rachel elbowed Henry. "Come on, let's check it out." They headed toward Kelvin, and then all three split up, searching for anything that could have made the light Frank Rosenbloom saw.

Henry looked for signs of a fire pit in the grass. "Maybe somebody started a bonfire that night," he said.

Rachel laughed. "To cook s'mores in a hailstorm? Keep dreaming."

Rachel looked through the gardens, making her way past a four-foot high replica of a lighthouse. She stopped at the ivy-covered lattice nearest to the car shelter. It stretched nearly ten feet up the house, giving the manor a nice old-world feel. From a distance, Henry saw her kneel down. "Hey," she called out. "Come quick."

Henry and Kelvin jogged over. She stared at the base of the lattice, which had planter boxes of dirt and roses to weigh it down. A long stretch of ground to the right looked indented, as if something heavy had recently been sitting there. She gave the ivy-covered decoration a knock. "I think someone moved this."

Henry nudged some of the vines aside, revealing blackened, charred siding.

"Stand back," Kelvin said. Grabbing the right side of the lattice, he pulled. As it slid, Henry stepped back. A long, deeply black, sinister-looking mark scarred the wooden siding where the lattice had been. It stood about eight feet tall, stretching up the house like a massive, terrible serpent.

"Whoa," Henry said.

Rachel ran her fingers over it. "Man, it's burnt."

Kelvin came forward to study it. He leaned close enough that his long nose almost touched the burnt wood. Henry crossed his arms, keeping his distance. "Was it lightning?"

Kelvin straightened up. "That's what we need to find out." He took a number of steps away from the house and, motioning for Henry and Rachel to follow, he pointed to the top of the house. "Do you see those? Those thin poles sticking out from the highest points on the roof?"

Henry and Rachel joined Kelvin and followed his finger, seeing two short black poles sticking out from the roof. One topped a rooster weather vane clasped to the largest of the dark-shingled spires, and the second stood farther away, affixed to the chimney. Two cleverly-hidden cables led from the rods down the back of the house.

Henry nodded. "Yeah. Lightning rods."

"Supposed to keep houses safe from lightning, right?" Rachel asked. "Maybe they're busted."

"We need to check." Kelvin jogged back to his car and, after a few minutes of rustling, returned with a small device attached to long wires. "This is an ohm meter. We can use it to test the lightning rods."

Henry turned his gaze to the tall spires, far above.

"The only problem," Kelvin said, "is that somebody needs to climb to the roof."

♀   ♀   ♀

Henry gripped the three-section, extendable ladder with both hands, helping Rachel and his uncle lug it from the car shelter. They planted it in the grass and, with Henry holding one side and Rachel steadying the other, Kelvin ascended toward the shiny gutter and dark shingles of the roof. Henry watched as one of the long wires of the ohm meter followed his uncle up. The other end of the wire trailed down into the device at Henry's feet. Kelvin placed a foot on the roof and, in the glare of the bright blue sky, stepped out of sight.

Henry brushed off his hands and picked up the ohm meter. He'd used it once before when he helped Kelvin test the lightning rods of a batty old lady in New York, so he knew how it worked. The woman had been convinced that her lightning rods were actually secret government equipment put there to monitor her thoughts. What a strange job that turned out to be.

The wire continued to snake up the side of the house; then it stopped. "All right, I'm here," Kelvin called out from far above.

Rachel jogged away from the house and gazed up at the roof. "He's at the first lightning rod, near that big rooster weathervane."

"Which one is that?" Henry asked.

"The left one."

Henry nodded, checking the device in his hands. It worked by sending out a small electric current. After Kelvin attached one wire to the top of the lightning rod and Henry attached the other to the cable that led down from it, it would form a loop, a complete circuit. The weak electric current from the device would simulate a miniature lightning strike. If the lightning rod was working properly, the electricity should flow freely from one wire to the other. Henry could monitor the result on the meter. If the rods were operating correctly, then lightning almost certainly didn't make the burn mark on the side of the house.

Henry knelt in flowers at the bottom end of the lightning rod cable. It took him several minutes to get set up. From out of sight, Kelvin's words drifted down to him and Rachel. "You two know who invented the lightning rod, right?"

Henry rolled his eyes. He could already tell this would be one of his uncle's tangents. But he held his tongue and focused on his task.

"Sure," Rachel called out. "Ben Franklin. One of our founding fathers. He helped start the US."

"Very good," Kelvin said. "Benjamin Franklin

wore many hats in his life, and I'm not talking about his coon-skin one either. He was a politician, a writer, a businessman, an inventor, and a scientist." Kelvin said that last word with a certain *oomph*, a majestic grandeur which was crystal clear even from a distance.

"Scientists," he went on, "are people who use their wits to discover things about the world around them, like we're doing now. A long time ago, you know, some people thought thunder was the sound of clouds crashing together. Others thought it was supernatural. They'd ring the church bells to try to ward lightning away. It took quite a few deaths before they decided the top of a bell tower wasn't the safest place to be in a thunderstorm."

Henry hadn't known that.

"All right," Kelvin called out. "My end is attached."

"Okay. Hold on." Henry touched his wire to the bottom of the lightning rod cable. The needle in the ohm meter flicked to the right. "Looks fine," he called out. "Let's do the other one."

"Sure," Kelvin said.

Momentarily, the wire leading up the house started moving again, apparently trailing Kelvin to the farther lightning rod. Kelvin continued his story.

"Ben Franklin was a clever one. He wanted to know more about lightning. He wondered whether lightning and electricity were the same thing, so he devised tests to find out. That's how science works. After coming up with an idea, you have to test it to see if you're right. That's the most important step: the testing."

Rachel stared up at the roof. "He tested his idea with a kite, right?"

Henry smiled, glad Rachel could put up with Kelvin's weirdness.

"In part," Kelvin said. "Ben fixed a wire to the top of a kite and a key to the bottom and went out in a thunderstorm. Lots of people say lightning struck the kite, but that simply isn't true. The wire just attracted a small amount of charge from the thunderstorm and when Ben brought his knuckle to the key, a small spark jumped to it. He trapped some of this electricity in a Leyden jar, which is a special apparatus used for storing static charge, and did more tests with it later. That's how he discovered lightning is just electricity. If lightning had struck his kite that day, we might have someone else on the hundred dollar bill."

Henry quivered. He pictured the stack of hundred dollar bills in the small white envelope two nights ago. Lightning, Kelvin had told him, is hot enough to melt sand into glass. The thought of anyone being struck by that, much less Ben Franklin—the pleasant, genial guy on the front of those bills—was a bit unnerving.

"But the point is this," Kelvin said. "Since lightning is electricity, it will take the easiest path to the ground. That usually means hitting the highest point of something, like up where I am now. And boy, it's breezy up here! If the lightning rod is here instead of a foolish detective, it will hit that, follow the wire, and go harmlessly into the ground."

"And since Ben figured out what lightning was..." Rachel started.

"He could figure out," Henry finished, "how to keep people safe from it."

Kelvin appeared at the edge of the roof. "All right, all set on my end."

Henry knelt down, touching his wire to the second cable. He looked at the reading on the device.

"Okay," he called out. "It's done."

Ben Franklin invented the lightning rod.

Sometimes he wore a coon-skin hat

writer

Businessman + Scientist

He must've been a cool dude in person (like Henry)

lightning touches down

Like Franklin, you should test your idea to see if it's right.

Henry and Rachel steadied the ladder again, and thirty seconds later Kelvin stepped back onto solid earth. Wiping his forehead, he coiled up the wires. "So?"

Henry held out the ohm meter. "Both rods are working perfectly."

Kelvin pressed his lips together. For a moment, nobody said a thing. They all turned and looked up at the long, serpentine burn mark on the back of the house. At last, Rachel said what they were all thinking. "Then lightning didn't make this mark."

Henry nodded. The black scorch loomed over them, stretching up the mansion. But the roof remained unmarked. Lightning would definitely have struck the roof first.

"Could you smell it for me, Henry?"

Henry twisted around to his uncle. "What?"

It surprised Henry to see his uncle looking a bit embarrassed. "This nose of mine doesn't work very well anymore," he said, "but I need to know what it smells like."

Kelvin had mentioned this once before, Henry now remembered. He handed the meter back to his uncle. Leaning forward, he put his nose to the dark, charred wood. "Smells like... burnt wood. Why?"

"No gasoline?"

"No."

Kelvin scratched the back of his neck. "No, of course not. Gasoline evaporates too readily. It would be long gone by now."

Rachel looked up from the scorch. "You sure someone set a fire?"

"Without a doubt. I've seen plenty of lightning strikes before, and this isn't one of them. The test only confirmed what I suspected from the beginning."

"Then who—" Henry began.

A muffled clanging crash, like a collection of pots falling off a shelf, echoed from beyond one of the second floor windows.

Henry took an involuntary step backward. "I thought no one was here!"

Kelvin stared at the window. "No one should be."

Chapter Ten

Letters in the Study

Henry's eyes shot to the car shelter. No new cars. No, of course not—he definitely would have heard someone arrive. So who made the noise? He ran forward, leaping through the shelter and rounding into the front yard, with Rachel and Kelvin just behind.

Empty. Nobody there either.

"Look!" Rachel pointed. One of the house's front windows, broken in the storm, stood open.

Henry felt a jolt in his chest. "That was definitely closed yesterday."

"Quiet," Kelvin ordered. They crept toward the window, listening. It opened into a dimly lit room. No sound came from inside. The house had only been empty a few days, but it seemed condemned and forgotten already.

Then, from somewhere deep inside, a solitary stair groaned.

Kelvin turned to Henry and Rachel, his features so stern that Henry recoiled. "Look, this is important. I want you two to stay out here, okay?"

When he got no answer, Kelvin repeated himself, more firmly this time. "Okay?"

Henry and Rachel nodded. Kelvin put his foot on the sill. "No matter what you hear, don't follow me in."

Kelvin slipped into the darkened house. The sound of footsteps on hardwood floor drifted back for a few seconds more, growing softer. Then silence.

Henry stepped to the window. Rachel joined him. Sunlight from outside illuminated a stirring of dust on the oaken floor. Tall mahogany bookcases stood in darkness along the left wall. On the adjacent wall a huge antique map of the world hung over an ornate desk. Papers and books lay in neat piles across the desk's surface. The room was a study, but one much more vast and grand than Kelvin's.

Henry concentrated on the doorway Kelvin had disappeared through. Beyond lay a hallway, then a second large room, its furniture silhouetted by curtained windows on the far wall.

No more sounds came from inside. Almost a minute passed. Henry turned to Rachel. She bit her lip.

"What if he needs help?" Henry said.

"He told us to stay put. It could be dangerous."

Henry's heart ached. Silence still emanated from

the window. He imagined some skilled intruder springing on Kelvin in the dark. He imagined poison gas, choking Kelvin in a closed room, or deadly darts sinking noiselessly into his neck. With nobody to help him, what chance did Kelvin have?

Regardless of what Kelvin had said, regardless of how serious he had looked, Henry couldn't just stand there and wait. He wasn't going to lose any family today. He put his foot on the windowsill.

"But..." Rachel started. Before she could finish, Henry dropped inside.

The room felt cooler than Henry had expected. The AC must never have been turned off. Good for the power company. Bad for Henry. The sudden chill of the study spoke of unseen, tentacled horrors lying in wait in every corner.

Henry stepped forward, glancing around the dim room. The corner to his left held things he hadn't seen from the window: a globe, a leather reading chair, a small fireplace. On the mantel above the fireplace sat a single blue and yellow porcelain bird, which looked as if it lacked a companion. Beside it lay a spot free of dust. A weird quietness hung over the room.

This felt wrong. Henry shouldn't be here. He should have listened to his uncle. He considered turning back.

But he couldn't just run away. He stepped toward the hallway door. The massive desk sat to his right, a piece of paper protruding from the central drawer. He stopped. The window gave just enough light to make out two large words, scrawled in red ink.

You shouldn't—

The words looked angry, threatening. Henry pulled the note out.

You shouldn't be here.

Henry stepped back. The note fluttered to the floor.

Rachel's voice came in from the window. "What? What is it?"

Henry wanted to run again, but his legs seemed stuck in place. Reaching down, he picked the note up.

You shouldn't be here.

That's all it said. On the back, nothing. Was it meant for him? Henry pulled the brass handle of the drawer. It slid open with oiled precision. Inside lay piles of papers and folders. Should he go help Kelvin? No, now that he thought about it, Kelvin could take care of himself and didn't need Henry up there getting in the way. Henry paged through a few of the documents. Mostly nothing. Banking records, employee registrars, business mail.

Then another note, in the same angry red hand as the first.

If you don't leave, you'll live to regret it.

Okay, definitely spooked now, Henry thought.

He looked around, half expecting to see the ghost of Edward Wrightly hovering in the corner, covered in tattered cloth and hailstone welts. But no, just an empty corner.

Henry eyed the note again. This one came in an envelope. Who was it addressed to? His hand trembling, he turned it over to see: *Henry Alabaster.*

Henry jumped. He looked again. No, not Henry Alabaster; his imagination had played a trick on him. What did it say? *Edward Wrightly.*

Henry let out a deep breath. Of course it wasn't meant for him. He held closer to his face, looking for a return address, but none existed. In the upper corner, a postmark covered the stamp. It was dated just over two weeks ago.

Henry put the note down and tried to breathe more steadily. He flipped through the other papers in the old desk. So many things filled the drawers, the fruitful and fruitless endeavors of a busy life.

Henry plunged into deeper layers. Near the bottom he uncovered another envelope, in the same angry hand as the others. This one looked much older. The postmark read June 16th of last year. One year ago, almost to the day.

Move, or else.

Henry stared at the message in the vast, lonely silence of the enormous house. Someone hadn't liked Edward Wrightly living here, that much was clear.

The pile of documents now lay strewn across the desk. The huge antique map of the world hung on the wall above. Here rested Edward Wrightly's work and endeavors, all abandoned, never to be finished. A whole life, just gone. It seemed cruel and pointless.

From far away, a crash shattered the silence of the house. Noises echoed to Henry through what sounded like cavernous rooms. In an instant he remembered why he had come inside.

Henry shoved the three notes deep inside his pants pocket. Shouts echoed toward him, then running footsteps. Henry stared at the door. Should he help, or leave?

A second passed. In the next, a figure rounded through the doorway with a flash of silver in his hands.

Henry didn't have time to react. The intruder slammed into him, knocking air from Henry's lungs and throwing him from his feet. Henry's head hit something solid. A weight crushed against his chest and his leg jolted with pain.

The weight lifted. Henry saw the intruder, a teen with messy blond hair, clamber through the window and leap outside.

Rachel shouted. Kelvin sprinted into the room.

"Henry!" Kelvin skidded to a halt, panting heavily. His wide eyes stared at Henry, then shot to the window.

Henry sat up with a great deal of effort. His uncle stepped to the windowsill, but no farther. Mashing his teeth together, Kelvin pounded the sill with his fist.

"I'm fine, I'm fine," Henry said. "Go!"

But Kelvin didn't go. He turned from the window with wild eyes.

It had been a lie anyway. Henry didn't feel fine. He felt as if he had been trampled. Leather-bound books lay on the floor around him. A few silver plates rested among them.

Silver plates? Those hadn't been on the bookshelf.

Henry looked up. His uncle stared at him from what seemed like a great height, fists clenched, breathing heavily. "What on earth are you doing in here, Henry? I told you to stay outside! Didn't you listen?"

Henry didn't know what to say. He felt small, and his cheeks burned. Kelvin stomped back to the window. Outside, Rachel spoke up. "Yeah, yeah, I'm fine. He just surprised me, that's all."

Henry rubbed his leg. His body ached all over and his chin throbbed, but otherwise he seemed intact—nothing broken, at least. Kelvin's legs paced back over. Even without looking up, Henry felt his uncle's gaze.

"Just what were you thinking, Henry?"

Henry still didn't look up.

"This is why I told you to stay outside. Are you all right?"

Henry's cheeks burned, his embarrassment turning to anger. "I'm fine." He felt like crying.

Kelvin knelt down. "I just want you to be safe. Listen to me next time. You could have been badly hurt."

Henry pushed his uncle's hands away. "I'm fine, okay? Don't be so concerned."

"I just want—" Kelvin started.

"I can take care of myself. Okay, Kelvin? Just go away. Don't pretend you're my father!"

Henry labored to his feet. He didn't know why he had said that.

Kelvin stayed quiet for a second more. He straightened up too. "I wasn't—"

"Forget it. It was my fault. I messed everything up."

Henry turned away and squeezed his eyes shut. Those tears were starting to come out. Why had he mentioned his dad?

For a moment, silence emanated from the spot where Kelvin stood. It somehow felt like a complete void, as if Kelvin had suddenly shriveled away and disappeared from existence. Several long seconds passed before he spoke. "Henry, I—"

"I said forget it!" Henry's cheeks burned, but the anger started to fade, leaving him with dizziness in his head and a stabbing pain in his leg. In the daylight outside, Rachel glanced away, pretending not to pay attention.

Henry still didn't turn around. He couldn't stand to look his uncle in the eye. Pain lingered in his uncle's silence.

A knock came at the windowsill. "You two about done?"

"Yeah," Henry said. He stepped toward the window. From behind came the sounds of Kelvin slowly putting things away. As Henry grabbed the window frame, Kelvin spoke up.

"Did you notice the kid?"

Henry didn't turn around. "What about him?"

"He was carrying these." Kelvin chimed two of the silver plates together.

"So he was a thief," Henry said. "So what?"

"A thief," Kelvin repeated, "and a teenager."

Kelvin was right. The boy was a teenager, just as Frank Rosenbloom had said. Still, Henry didn't reply. He didn't want to talk to his uncle right now. His cheeks felt hot. He didn't want to be in this awful room for even another second.

Henry put his foot onto the windowsill. As he did, something crinkled in his pants pocket, but his head was so full of anger and embarrassment that he couldn't figure out what it was.

Chapter Eleven

Isabel and Eugene

Henry dropped to the grass. His leg flared with pain, jolting his last thought, whatever it had been, out of his head. In front of him, Rachel stood in the bright sunlight of the front yard, her arms folded tightly. She looked nervous and unhappy. "You all right?"

Henry nursed his leg with one hand and his head with the other. "Yeah, I'm okay."

After a moment, Kelvin stepped through the window. His eyes stayed fixed to the northwest, staring out over the long yard and across the street.

"The burglar went that way," Rachel explained. "I lost track of him behind the houses."

Kelvin strode away and flipped open his phone. He spoke with a police officer on the other end, and then pushed the window firmly shut. "We'll find that kid sooner or later."

Rachel rubbed her forehead. "You think he was

involved with the fire?"

"I can't say. I would have liked to ask him some questions. Like Benjamin Franklin when he was studying lightning, we need to know a bit more before we can unravel this mystery."

Henry shriveled. If he hadn't gone inside the house, they'd probably be questioning that kid right now. He had to change the subject. "Let's talk to the neighbors. Maybe they can tell us something."

All three of them looked down the long, shallow slope of the lawn toward the weathered houses on the far side of the street. A bright look came into Rachel's eyes. "Oh, I know."

Reaching into her pants pocket, Rachel pulled out a small, worn notebook and a pen. Turning to a blank page, she began sketching lines and boxes. A map of the neighborhood soon covered the page. "There, now it should be easier to keep track of everyone."

Curiosity nudged aside Henry's anger. The map looked pretty much perfect. "Where'd you learn to do that, Rachel?"

"Class." Rachel grinned mischievously. "Course, we were supposed to be writing essays. Hey, Kelvin, do you have a compass?" Kelvin produced a compass from his coat pocket, and Rachel added two things to her drawing. "A compass rose and a scale. Any good map needs 'em."

Kelvin smiled. He told Rachel the names of the

Isabel and Eugene

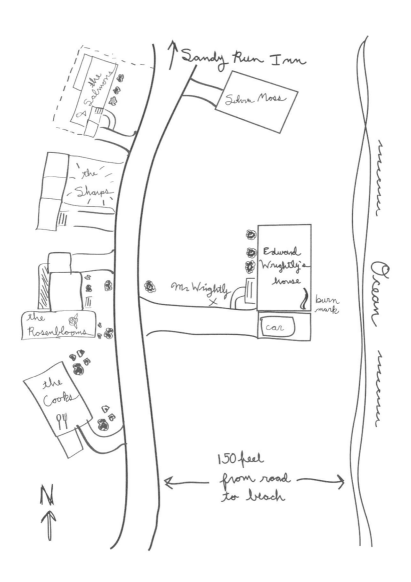

105

neighbors and she wrote them beside the houses. From north to south: Elena and Rodger Salmon, Victoria and Walter Sharp, Frank and Josephina Rosenbloom, Eugene and Isabel Cook. The only name Henry didn't recognize was Silvia Moss, which Kelvin told Rachel to write beside a large house to the north. He turned and stared at that large, quiet place in the distance, but he didn't want to talk to his uncle, so he didn't ask about it.

"The other neighbors weren't in town on the night of the death," Kelvin said, "so we'll rule them out as suspects for now and focus on the people who were here. You two take notes as we go. We'll compare clues later to make sure we don't miss anything."

Rachel nodded. The corners of her map quivered in the afternoon breeze. Henry stared at it, studying the geography of the neighborhood.

"There." He pointed to one house in particular. "Eugene and Isabel Cook had the best view of the fire. Maybe they saw who started it."

Across the distant street stood the Cooks' house, a tan, two-story building with a wooden seagull mounted on the front. Kelvin stared at it, then turned and looked toward the corner where the fire had burned. "That's true. But they already told us they were gone that night."

Henry's enthusiasm sagged.

"Although," Kelvin said, "their driveway is the

only one with a car in it, so they might be our only choice."

Rachel closed her notebook. "Then let's do it."

Together, they marched down the long, grassy lawn to the street below. Henry's leg still hurt a little with each step, and he held his hand up to the blazing sun. The sea breeze wasn't doing much to help today. In front, Kelvin wore his long tan overcoat and hat, not seeming to mind the heat at all.

They crossed into the Cooks' driveway. The blue sedan sitting there had the same pockmarked look as Mr. Wrightly's car. Henry rubbed his fingers over the dents as he passed. If hail could do that to a car, what could it do to a person? he wondered. At the front door, Kelvin rapped his knuckles against recently painted wood.

A few seconds passed. With a shudder, the door opened. On the other side stood Eugene Cook, the portly, southern figure from yesterday evening, paintbrush in hand. White paint streaked his forehead and fresh drops dotted his long seersucker clothes.

"Well ain't that the berries. Mr. McCloud, isn't it? Good to see y'all again so soon." He wiped a long sleeve across his brow and looked down at himself. "Pardon the appearance."

"Good afternoon, Mr. Cook," Henry said.

"Hi," Kelvin said cheerily. "Do you have a

moment?"

"Well, for you lot, sure I do! Make yourselves at home. And please, it's Eugene."

All three stepped into the cool house. Rachel stared at Eugene's clothes. "So what's with you?"

Mr. Cook chuckled. "Renovations, darlin'. Just one of those things Isabel's been botherin' me about. We mean to rent this place out, see, so it needs to look slicker than snot, pardon the expression. It'll have a wonderful view, and we think people will really take a shine to it."

Eugene led them down the hallway past freshly painted doors to the dining room. Motioning to a set of hardwood chairs around the dinner table, he promptly disappeared, returning a minute later with glasses and a tall pitcher of lemonade. Henry grabbed a glass.

"So what brings you folks round today?" Eugene asked, sitting down on the arm of a chair.

Isabel appeared at his side, tightly wrapped in dark sweats and a blue-green bathrobe. "Have you found out something new about the storm, Mr. McCloud?"

Kelvin rested his wide-brimmed hat on his knee and filled a glass with lemonade. "We're working on it, ma'am. Actually, I was hoping you could help. The lightning must have been spectacular that night. We think it struck Mr. Wrightly's house and started a fire."

"A fire?" Eugene and Isabel responded in unison, Eugene's southern drawl mixing with Isabel's more dulcet tone.

"Just a small one," Henry clarified.

"Happened around nine fifteen, we think," Rachel said.

Isabel glanced between them, a look of shock lingering on her refined but pallid features. "Begging your pardon, but I don't know a thing about it."

Eugene nodded sadly. "Sorry to tell y'all."

Henry noticed the corners of his uncle's mouth drop. Behind Kelvin, a large window opened into the Cooks' front yard. Edward Wrightly's house sat out on the slight rise in the distance, vast and silent. Shame the Cooks hadn't been home. They had an ideal view.

Henry took a sip of lemonade. The cold liquid had already made water condense on the outside of the glass. Across from him, Rachel asked, "You were at a movie, right, Mr. Cook? See anything good?"

"Jaws, darlin'. Nice little theater, like Isabel and I used to go to in Alabama. They're doin' classic movies this week." Eugene pressed his lips together. "Had to go by my lonesome, though. The usual gang didn't fancy venturing out in the weather. I may be able to find what's left of my ticket, if y'all wanted to see."

Kelvin shrugged. "If you want."

Eugene left the room. A few moments of rustling and cursing later, he returned with an orange stub of paper, torn in half. "Here you are. Jaws, eight o'clock. Storm knocked out the power around ten, just before the end. Couldn't drive home the way it was howlin' neither, so I didn't get back till well after midnight. Stood by my car and watched the storm till it passed."

Henry took the stub and looked it over. Jaws, 8:00 p.m.

"And you were at the book club, right?" Rachel asked Isabel. "Pay much attention to the storm?"

"I'd say so! It was pretty hard not to. Eugene had the car, so the girls and I decided to make a night of it. It was a bit thrilling, bless my soul. All our talk about Dracula and vampires made it hard to sleep in a new place, especially with the storm kicking about outside. And just after we turned out the lights, around ten thirty, I suppose, one of the windows shattered. Hail smashed it right open!"

"Elena Salmon was present, right?" Kelvin asked.

"Sure was. Silvia Moss too, if you've met her—a nervous dear, she is." Isabel sniffled, then clarified. "Though Elena left around eight. She made a few phone calls, then stormed out. Didn't see her again after that."

Henry leaned forward. "What were the calls

about?"

Here came an extended pause, punctuated by a sneeze. "She wanted to call her husband. Nobody picked up, so she called some bar, I think. She didn't say anything, but afterward she left the room. Don't think I was eavesdropping, dear, but I heard some yelling about money, and when she stomped out, she was cross as a lowercase *t*."

Across the table, Rachel shot Henry a meaningful look. He gave a slight nod, picturing Elena and Rodger arguing in the alley. If only he knew what that argument was about.

"Mrs. Cook," Rachel asked, "what did Elena think of Mr. Wrightly? Were they friends?"

"Friends? Well sure. Not sure why you ask but, out of any of us, Elena probably liked the old man the best."

"What about her husband, Rodger?" Henry probed.

"What do you mean?"

"Well, did Rodger ever say anything bad about Mr. Wrightly? Did Rodger, you know, hate him?"

The question caught Isabel off guard. She lowered the handkerchief from her mouth. Beside her, still perched on the arm of his chair in his paint-smeared seersuckers, Eugene started to flush.

"Now, young sir and miss," he said, "I'm not sure what any of this has to do with that storm you're investigatin', but Rodger Salmon is a good ol' friend of mine. He could have hated Ed Wrightly. He could have loved him. It doesn't matter. He didn't have nothin' to with what happened that night."

"Apologies," Kelvin said. "These kids have a bad habit of getting off topic sometimes."

Eugene breathed heavily. "Rodger's a good friend of mine, that's all. You can't just go around implyin'—"

He didn't get chance to finish. A sudden clang of metal and a hiss came from around the hallway. Everyone jumped. Eugene nearly fell from his armrest. A long-haired brown and black cat, dripping with white paint, shot across the dining room and out through the kitchen door.

"That infernal cat!" roared Eugene, leaping to his feet. He bounded through the kitchen and disappeared. Isabel tried to give a polite smile, coughed, and then she and Kelvin vanished after her husband.

Henry and Rachel looked at each other. Footsteps resounded through far rooms. Angry hisses followed, then much shouting, then some curses from Eugene that Henry had never heard before.

The clatter mounted the stairs. Rachel and Henry rose from their seats, but didn't follow. The dull thud of footsteps continued on the floor above, running this way, then the other.

Henry looked away from the ceiling. Rachel

wasn't beside him anymore. She had crept into the hallway.

"What are you doing?" Henry whispered.

"Investigating," Rachel replied. "It's what we're supposed to be doing, right?"

"But what about— "

"There's nothing to worry about this time, Henry. I just want to look." She righted the overturned can of paint in the hall, jumped over the slowly growing white puddle, and disappeared through a door.

Henry stepped from one foot to the other. But what else could he do? He followed Rachel. If they got in trouble for this one, he wasn't going to let her face it alone.

Rachel stood in the middle of a guest bedroom. Several large paintings adorned the walls. A sink lay upside down on the floor. Henry jumped the hallway puddle and followed Rachel in, inspecting the white enamel sink. The faucet handles were shaped like seagulls. Beyond a second doorway, white plastic pipes and a tool bag sat on a bathroom floor.

Rachel turned to one of the large paintings. It showed a forest of thin and elegant trees, with soft light filtering down through the leaves. "It's signed E. Cook," she said, waving Henry over. "I think Eugene did these. They're really good. Maybe I should ask him for drawing tips sometime."

"I don't think you need any tips," Henry replied.

She laughed, turning away.

Henry kept looking. Four other paintings hung on the walls. A small boat drifted out on a dark lake in one, and the other three, definitely the best of the bunch, showed golden sunrises.

The commotion upstairs died away. Henry motioned to Rachel. "Come on. You can admire the art some other time."

Henry made for the hallway. A small picture frame on the dresser by the door caught his attention. In the photo, Eugene and Isabel Cook stood with Rodger and Elena Salmon at the beach.

"Look how happy they are," Rachel said.

"Yeah." Henry narrowed his eyes. This marked the first time he had seen Elena Salmon look happy. In the picture, she hugged Rodger with sweet affection. Beside them, fishing poles leaned against a blue cooler, and a sandy beach stretched into the distance behind. Rodger stared at something out of frame. Eugene and Isabel both smiled widely.

Henry turned the frame over. On the back was a note. *Aug. 17. Fishing with the Salmons.*

Henry flipped to the front. "They definitely look like good friends."

Rachel stayed silent. She gave Henry a tap. He looked up. Eugene Cook stood in the doorway, breathing heavily and even more paint-splattered than before.

"What are you two doing in here?"

Seeing the photo, he took it from Henry's hands.

"This here is private, you know. You can't just go snooping around someone's house."

Henry took a step back.

Eugene brushed past him and strode into the room, inspecting the sink and the small bathroom.

"There are renovations goin' on in here, you know. It could be dangerous, and I don't want y'all messing anything up."

"I like your paintings, Mr. Cook," Rachel said.

Eugene glanced up. "Well, I appreciate the compliment, darlin', but you still don't belong in here." He pushed them out of the room and drew the door shut. "You're guests here. Next time, mind your manners."

A hiss sounded at the end of the hall. Kelvin and Isabel appeared, Kelvin holding the cat against his now-only-mostly-tan overcoat. A thorough frown crinkled beneath his hawkish nose.

Eugene stepped across the white puddle on the floor and strode down the hall, yanking at a towel from the linen closet. "Thank you, Mr. McCloud," he said, taking the paint-covered cat. "Now if y'all would excuse us, Isabel should get back to bed and I have a whole lick of messes to attend to. It's been a pleasure having you here."

As he looked between his three guests, a long strand of white paint dripped from his dark hair.

Henry, Rachel, and Kelvin made for the door.

Before leaving, however, they asked a few last questions. Dripping with paint and holding the squirming, hissing cat in his arms, Eugene answered.

"No," he said, "I don't know where Elena Salmon stormed off to that night."

"No," he said next, "I can't say I saw anyone else at the theater."

"Yes," he said finally, "I sure do know where Victoria Sharp was that night. She was at the bank, working late."

"At least," Isabel added with a sneeze, "that's what she told us."

And with this, Eugene and Isabel herded their guests through the door and firmly shut it. The lock clicked into place behind.

Out in the sunlight again, Kelvin stared down at his overcoat.

"Well ain't that the berries," he muttered.

Where before it had been a clean, professional tan, it now bore a large white splotch—one which looked immediately, and undeniably, like a cat.

Chapter Twelve

Deeper and Deeper

After leaving the Cooks' house, Henry, Rachel, and Kelvin didn't go right back to the hotel. Instead, trudging past the late Edward Wrightly's mansion, they descended to the rough sands and breaking waves of the beach, and there they sat on the sand and discussed the mysteries of the case.

More and more, it was becoming clear that the people of this town had secrets. The argument in the alleyway, the fire at the estate, Elena's abrupt departure from the book club—all of these things pointed toward a larger picture, a picture that none of the neighbors seemed able, or willing, to explain.

Henry thought about this puzzle, but found time for other things, too. Leaning over to Rachel, he pointed out the gentle curve of the ocean's blue-green horizon in the distance—the curve of the earth. A bright look came into her eyes. Pulling out her notebook, Rachel started to sketch all the little details of the beach.

Kelvin, sitting a few feet away, tried to scrape the cat paint off of his coat with a seashell.

And in this manner, with the shadow of the dead man's mansion gradually creeping down the beach toward the three detectives, the rest of the afternoon passed into evening.

Once back at the hotel, Henry and Rachel parted ways. Henry and Kelvin ordered Chinese food and ate it as they sat on their beds, watching an action movie on the flickering hotel TV. An awkward silence hung between them.

Henry thought about the study. The words he'd yelled at his uncle rang in his head. Why did he do that? He thought about the notes in the desk. The notes! Henry felt his pocket. They were still there. Henry opened his mouth to tell Kelvin, but then closed it again. All he could think about was being in that study, sitting bruised on the floor, yelling at Kelvin. A lump rose in his throat. He went into the bathroom to brush his teeth.

Kelvin flicked off the TV. "Goodnight, Henry."

A moment passed. "Goodnight."

The awkward silence returned. Henry slipped back into bed and Kelvin turned off the light. After a while, Henry heard snoring.

Henry turned on his side. The hot smarting of sunburn made him shiver slightly.

The sun. The thought drifted through Henry. Even in the cool hotel room, AC kicked into high gear, the warm pain made him imagine being out there again, sitting on the beach by the dead man's house, baking in the sun. Kelvin never had this problem. Kelvin loved sunscreen, but Henry couldn't stand the cold, wet feeling of putting the stuff on. Maybe he'd have to reconsider. A brief chill would be miles better than a long burn.

Henry turned to his other side. The sunburn rang out again.

The sun. Over the past eight months, Kelvin had told Henry many things about the sun. Right now, one conversation in particular nagged at Henry's mind. It had been at bedtime one night, with Kelvin sitting on the edge of Henry's bed.

"Imagine," Kelvin said, "that you're in a spaceship."

Good way to start a story, Henry remembered thinking.

"Now, it doesn't have to be a realistic spaceship," Kelvin had continued. "It can be a small, sleek one, like the one here on your nightstand." He tapped on Henry's spaceship alarm clock. "You're the captain of this ship, and you're looking out of the cockpit at Earth. It's this serene blue and green sphere sitting there in space, surrounded by a vast blackness dotted with stars. White clouds sweep gradually around it. The atmosphere is just a thin layer, like the skin on an apple, yet vitally important. Can you picture it?"

Sitting in his bed, covers over his knees, Henry nodded.

"Deep in the distance beyond is a bright glare. That glare is the sun, a great furnace of hydrogen and helium gases. It's very far from the earth and almost unimaginably huge. You could put a hundred Earths side by side and the sun would still be wider. This is what the earth orbits. We're kept from drifting off into the far reaches of space by the sun's gravitational pull. All matter in the universe pulls towards each other, you know. That's what we call gravity." He tapped on his chest, and then tapped on Henry's. "Even you and I, right now, are pulling on Pluto, just as it pulls on us."

Henry remembered smiling at this. Somehow, it made him feel closer to his parents. No matter where they were, he thought, he'd never be cut off from them completely.

"As for the sun," Kelvin went on, "it's a star, just like the ones you see outside, speckling the night sky. The only difference is that this one is much closer. This is our star. It heats the earth with its rays, making life possible for us."

Henry nodded. He'd often wondered about other planets and possibly other life in the distant reaches of space, but sometimes he overlooked the wonders closer to home. Kelvin readjusted himself on the side of the bed and continued.

"This energy from the sun—this radiation—heats the earth, but not evenly. Places near the equator receive sunlight more directly, while light at the poles hits the ground at an angle and gets spread out."

"That's why the equator is so much hotter, right?"

Kelvin smiled, the skin at the corners of his eyes crinkling up. "Precisely! And because the equator is so much warmer, some of its heat starts to move toward the poles. That may not sound very exciting, but it happens in two very interesting ways."

Kelvin paused here, grinning, for dramatic effect.

"The first way is through the ocean. Heat is transported in the system of colossal currents that circulate through the earth's vast oceans. The second way is through the atmosphere. And do you know how this happens?"

Henry shrugged.

"It's the weather."

Henry closed his eyes, thinking about this. "Weather is heat being moved?"

"Well, parts of the weather, I should say. Rain and hurricanes and trade winds and westerlies and all of those interesting things only occur because the atmosphere takes heat from warm places and eventually, slowly, and with many stops along the way, moves it closer to cold places. The exact details are all very complicated, because the earth is a complex place, but, at its heart, that's where weather comes from: the uneven heating of the earth. The sun, 93 million miles away, is the furnace that sets all of this in motion. If it weren't for the sun, weather on earth would basically never change. No wind, no rain, no anything, and that wouldn't be very interesting at all!"

Henry grinned. "If we didn't have a sun, I think we might have bigger problems than boring weather."

Kelvin laughed. "Yes, it's certainly important to us as well. So thank goodness for the sun."

Saying this, Kelvin put his hands on his knees and rose to his feet. "Now it's time for bed." He pulled Henry's thick cotton covers up to his shoulders and patted him on the knee. "And don't worry, tomorrow night I'll have a better bedtime story."

Kelvin walked to the door. With a quick goodnight, he turned off the light and left the room.

That night had been five months ago. As Henry now listened to his uncle's snores in the cool hotel room, a deep and sincere pain rose in his chest. Despite all of Kelvin's shortcomings, and despite his prickly nature and eccentricities, he had really been very good to Henry.

As good a replacement as Henry could have hoped.

Henry stared at the ceiling. Now he knew why he had yelled at Kelvin today. It wasn't that he hated his uncle, or disliked being looked after or told stories late at night. It was simply that Kelvin was no substitute for his parents. Henry didn't. want a substitute. He wanted his parents back.

If he closed his eyes, he could almost imagine his parents were with him now.

Henry's father, Arthur, had taught him how to throw a football and had shown him, on one long, lazy day together out on the lake, how to fish.

And, when he was younger, it had been his mother, Susan, not Kelvin, who sat on the end of his bed and told him stories. She told him tales of pirates and mermaids and monstrous sea creatures, and he fell asleep dreaming of huge waves crashing against his barnacled ship, fearless comrades at his shoulder, and untold adventure on the horizon ahead. Kelvin's stories were always told with care, of course, but his mother's were filled with love.

Henry pictured his parents—his father's short brown curls and round spectacles, and his mother's smile, her kind green eyes, and her long blond hair.

A warm, pleasant feeling rose in Henry's chest. His mind lingered on that golden blond hair for a moment more.

Before he figured out what it reminded him of, he drifted away to sleep.

Why we
have weather:

sunlight

Sunlight heats up the
area around the equator mostly.
The sun doesn't heat up
the North + South Pole very much.
        Heat differences like this
set the weather in motion.

equator

Henry opened his eyes, still heavy with sleep. Soft light came in through the hotel window. The sheets from the other bed lay rumpled on the floor, and Kelvin was gone.

Henry turned over. His leg hurt again and his back still burned dully. The door to the hallway stood open an inch. Voices and sounds of movement came from outside.

"What does it mean?" one of the voices said.

"You should call the police, dude," said another.

Henry sat up. He ran a hand through his hair and rubbed his eyes.

"Now, nobody panic," another voice said. "I'm sure there's nothing to worry about."

This voice was Kelvin's. Henry slid out of bed and pulled the door farther open. On the other side, a large man in a suit turned and looked at Henry with deeply set eyes.

Henry stepped into the hallway. He found Kelvin standing in his cloudy pajamas, surrounded by the large businessman and several others.

"What's going on?" Henry asked, rubbing his eyes.

Kelvin stopped talking. Without a word, he pointed back toward the door.

Henry looked. A glint of sharp metal made him jump. Not two feet from where he stood, a long, polished steak knife pierced the splintered wood of the doorframe. The serrated blade impaled a scrap of paper. On it, three words had been scrawled in red.

Leave. Or else.

Henry recognized the angry red writing at once. He took a step back, his back running into the wall. His eyes went to Kelvin. "Where'd it come from?"

"Don't know. Nobody saw who put it there."

Vanessa Willowby, Rachel's mother, stood opposite Kelvin, her dark features taut and anxious. "I found it, Henry. Clarence and I had a little break in our work, so I came to invite you two to breakfast. Scared me half to death."

The businessman with the deeply set eyes talked on his phone. "Yes, that's right. Sandy Run Inn, room, uh… room 327."

"Maybe it was a prank, dude," said a younger man with messy hair and beach-bum shorts. "You know, just some dweeb having a laugh."

A scowl hung on Kelvin's features. "Unlikely. I think someone wants us gone."

The businessman put his phone away. "The police will be here shortly."

Kelvin nodded. Raising his voice, he addressed the group as a whole. "Attention everyone, listen up. Thank you for your concern, but I think the police, Mrs. Willowby, and I can handle things from here on out."

The group shot curious and annoyed looks at Kelvin. The businessman puffed his cheeks, clearly upset he should be told to leave just when things were getting interesting. But eventually they all shuffled away, leaving Henry, Kelvin, and Vanessa together in the paisley hallway.

Vanessa looked drained, but she straightened herself with an admirable show of resolve. "I'm not sure what I can do, Kelvin, but I'll help however I can."

Kelvin studied the note, not looking at her. "Just tell the police what you know. I need to figure out where this thing came from."

Reluctantly, Henry's eyes returned to the note as well. Those angry red letters. Without a word, he stepped back into the hotel room. He found his shorts from yesterday. The notes from Mr. Wrightly's study remained crammed in the pocket, wrinkled but intact. Henry took a deep breath. He should have shown these to Kelvin last night. Dragging himself back out into the hall, he offered the notes to his uncle.

Kelvin's first expression showed curiosity. As he looked at the notes, it turned to astonishment. Then his long eyebrows lowered and those sharp gray eyes stared into Henry. "Henry," he said slowly, "where did you find these?"

Henry's cheeks burned. He didn't want to have this conversation. "In the study," he said, without explaining. "Yesterday."

Kelvin's attention remained fixed on Henry for

several seconds more, but he said nothing. Henry heard his own voice from yesterday, yelling at Kelvin.

Kelvin returned his eyes to the notes, turning them over in his hand. Vanessa leaned in to look. "What are they?"

Kelvin didn't reply. The scowl on his face deepened. He lifted one of the notes up to the one gouged into their doorframe by the long steak knife.

Henry looked away. He already knew the answer.

Kelvin lowered his hand. "It's a match."

Vanessa gasped. "Wait, so there really is... I mean, Rachel told me, but I didn't think..."

She didn't go on. Together, Henry and the two adults stared at the note, stuck in the doorframe by the long, serrated steak knife. Henry didn't need to be told what this meant. It meant Henry and Kelvin now found themselves in a sinking ship— the same ship, unfortunately, that Mr. Wrightly had been in.

Whoever had threatened Mr. Wrightly with those awful, angry notes didn't want a weather detective in Sandy Run.

The police were still pacing around, knocking on doors and asking questions, when Rachel and her father appeared.

"What in the world..." Clarence started to say.

"Mom!" Rachel cried, running forward. "You said you'd be back in a minute."

Henry and Vanessa did their best to soothe fears. Nobody had died, nobody was hurt. The police walked past again, following Kelvin. Henry grabbed Rachel's hand and led her into the hotel room, where they sat on Henry's unmade bed. An uneasy look glimmered in Rachel's eyes. "You're not going to leave because of this, are you?"

Henry didn't answer. He didn't know. Through the open door, he heard Vanessa and Clarence arguing about keeping Rachel safe.

"Your parents will still let us hang out, right?" Henry asked. "You know, despite the threats and everything?"

Rachel nodded. "Yeah, Dad worries, but Mom is tough. And she hates bullies. She'll like your uncle more after all this. Are you scared?"

Henry had a jittery feeling throughout his whole body, but he didn't want to tell Rachel that. "No," he said firmly, "and we're not leaving. We have a murder to solve."

Seeing Rachel relax a little at these words, he did too. They lay back on the bed, letting their heads hang off the side. Through the window beyond Rachel, Henry saw a gray, cloudy sky. He grabbed his barometer from the nightstand.

His intuition proved right. Under the scratched glass, the needle had swung much farther to the left. The pressure had dropped a lot since yesterday.

"I think it's going to storm today," he said.

Rachel took the barometer and held it in front of herself. "Nothing we can't handle."

They smiled at each other.

A sharp clap resounded at the door. "Come on, both of you, we're going to brunch."

Henry saw Vanessa Willowby standing in the doorway, upside-down. He and Rachel turned over. Behind Vanessa were Kelvin and Clarence, the latter sagging tiredly. The police had left.

Vanessa Willowby entertained no argument. Twenty-six minutes later the five of them sat at a small outdoor deli near the beach. Less than a block away, a boardwalk ran along the sand. People talked and laughed as they walked between the shops. In the other direction stretched a more businesslike side of town. A few stores lined the road, and in the distance, emptier streets branched off between brick and concrete buildings.

Still, the place felt nice. Despite his lingering feelings of guilt, Henry tried to enjoy the distant sound of crashing waves and the wholesome smell of salt water in the ocean air. He leaned back and thought. The ocean, still cool from the night, was keeping the air above it from getting too hot. That air blew onto the coast as a sea breeze. Behind the clouds, sunlight scattered off nitrogen and oxygen molecules, making the sky blue. And the sun, out there in space, set everything in motion.

Everything, Henry thought, including the storm currently on its way to Sandy Run.

To Henry's left at the white patio table, Kelvin sat picking at his overcoat. The cat spot hadn't come out in the wash, but simply faded. Now the long smear looked less like a cat and more like a cat's spirit. Henry leaned over and nudged Rachel.

"Hey," he whispered, "I think we finally found our ghost."

She laughed.

As brunch arrived—a pleasing assortment of waffles and pastries—conversation settled in. The police, it turned out, might not be much help. They assured Kelvin they would investigate this morning's threat, but they wouldn't comment about Mr. Wrightly's death.

"Let us do our job, Mr. McCloud," they said, taking the threatening notes with them as they left. "We'll look into it."

Still, Kelvin's investigation would continue. "We can't let a murderer intimidate us into leaving," he said, giving the patio table a heavy thump with his fist.

Vanessa gave a hearty, "Hear, hear!" and proposed a toast with her orange juice.

Afterward, Kelvin leaned over and told Henry about some phone calls he placed that morning. "I talked to Sylvia Moss. Nervous woman. She verified that she attended the neighborhood book club on the night of the storm. I then called the theater Eugene Cook went to. It lost power at ten, just like he said. As for Victoria Sharp, a coworker at the bank told me she was there until eleven that night. A man came in to see her around eight. Didn't leave until late."

"A man? Who?"

"The woman I spoke to didn't recognize him. He was tall, and left through the hail. He kept ranting about losing his savings gambling on baseball."

"Baseball, huh? What about the knife in our door?"

"Common kitchen knife. I doubt there will be any fingerprints."

"And Mr. Wrightly's missing umbrella? Do the police have that?"

"No. I suspect it's long gone by now."

"Weird. Ever hear back about Mr. Wrightly's will?"

"Yes, in fact. Everything Wrightly owned is going to charity except the house. It's going to be made into a bed and breakfast. I'm not sure if other people know that, but we should assume so. The attorney was all too happy to tell me."

As pleasantries continued, Henry leaned his head back. Beyond the large red and white umbrella that spouted from the table, gray clouds drifted across the sky. Just cumulus clouds for now, but things would get much worse before long.

The bill soon came. "Of course you're not paying," Clarence said, snatching the bill from Kelvin. "Our treat." A few minutes later, they all walked down the sidewalk past shops, heading for the car.

"Oh, let's look in here," Vanessa said at one window. Thick nets, barometers, and compasses hung on the walls of a nautical-themed shop. Kelvin trailed the Willowbys in, but Henry and Rachel stayed outside.

Henry glanced around. The business side of town stretched down the road. Three gulls landed nearby and Henry and Rachel made faces at them. A group of twenty-somethings walked by with a stroller. Beneath the cover, a baby grimaced.

Farther away, more people walked along the street. An old couple with ice cream, a group of kids, and—

Henry jumped. A woman with long blond hair was walking away.

As soon as he saw her, Henry knew. It was the woman from New York. That familiar snake began to coil in his gut, the same snake he had felt every morning since his parents disappeared.

"Kelvin," he called out. He looked into the store. Kelvin, Vanessa, and Clarence weren't in sight.

"What is it, Henry?" Rachel asked.

Henry didn't answer. "Kelvin!" he yelled.

No response. Henry turned back to the woman.

She was looking right at him.

She had heard.

Henry only caught a glimpse. Not enough to see a face. The woman whipped her head around and began to hurry away.

Henry had the sudden sensation of slipping into icy water, of trying to gasp for air just beneath the waves and getting only salt and spray. A lost, sputtering hopelessness. He was going to lose her again. He gave a last futile look into the store, and then turned to Rachel. She looked him straight in the eyes.

"That's her?"

Henry nodded.

"Then it's now or never."

She held out her hand. Henry gripped it and they began to run. They ran away from the storefront, away from Kelvin and Vanessa and Clarence, all probably looking at knick-knacks somewhere in the back, and dodged past tourists down that dirty and busy street.

With the pavement flying underfoot, they made for the corner where the blond-haired woman had, seconds before, disappeared.

Chapter Thirteen

The Alleys of Sandy Run

Rachel and Henry rounded the corner in a wild run, narrowly avoiding a young couple on the far side. Henry stumbled, caught himself, and looked through the people on the cobbled street.

The woman from New York ran past parents and children ahead.

"Wait!" Henry cried out. "Stop!"

The woman didn't even look back. Leaping through traffic, she disappeared through a pair of heavy wooden doors on the far side of the street. Dropping hands, Henry and Rachel waved for the cars to stop, then ran after her.

"Why's she running?" Rachel shouted.

Between gulps of air, Henry shouted back. "Don't know!"

Rachel heaved the thick wooden door open. The place seemed exceptionally dark. A waitress stood behind a booth. She opened her mouth to speak.

Henry spoke first. "The blond woman. Where'd she go?"

The waitress's mouth stayed open, her bubbly greeting stuck in her throat. She pointed left, between tables of cheerful people eating lunch. Henry and Rachel hurried that way.

"Thanks!" Rachel called back.

Henry searched through the restaurant, which had portraits of classic actors and actresses covering the paneled walls. Noise and commotion filled the place, but there was no sign of the woman. He and Rachel checked the booths. A series of surprised and scornful expressions greeted them, mouths half full of food.

"The door!" Rachel said.

At the back of the restaurant, through the kitchen, light poured in through the open fire escape. An irritated busboy strode over to close it, but Henry and Rachel got there first.

They leapt outside, shielding their eyes from the sudden brightness. A sliver of sun peeked from between clouds and illuminated the dented, overflowing dumpsters of the narrow alley.

Henry looked to his right, then spun to the left.

"There!" Rachel said. At the far end of the alley, the woman fled toward a wider street. That long blond hair bounced wildly on her shoulders. She glanced back and Henry made out a slight nose and wide eyes, but it was a fleeting, blurry look.

Henry tried to call out. A word formed on his lips. "Mo—"

It wouldn't come out. Why had that word leapt into his mind anyway?

Rachel grabbed his arm. "Come on! What're you waiting for?"

Adrenaline pumped through Henry's veins again. He and Rachel surged forward. They shot like Roman candles toward the end of the alleyway, running over trash and loose pavement. The blond woman made it to the street and slipped out of sight.

Henry and Rachel emerged from the alley a moment later, looking wide-eyed at the people on the street. Buildings and lampposts lined the sidewalk in either direction and the flat expanse of ocean lay in the distance.

Where had the woman gone?

Henry ran forward. He couldn't see her. More alleyways branched off from the road. Henry glanced down the first few, but each just led into some dreary distance. Had the woman really escaped him again?

"Come on," he said. "This way."

Henry ran down the nearest alley, Rachel not far behind. The sound of their footsteps echoed off the narrow brick walls. At the first intersection, they picked a direction and kept going. A mangy dog looked up and snarled as they passed, but didn't pursue. Next intersection, they turned again. The woman must have gone somewhere.

Henry's breathing quickened. His legs and lungs ached. He turned another corner, then a final one. He jumped a puddle, stumbled, and scraped his hands. Rising to his feet, he stared down a narrow, deserted street, an utterly unfamiliar place. Impersonal buildings reached toward the gray sky on both sides. There was no point in going any farther.

Rachel jogged up behind, breathing heavily. "Sorry."

Henry clenched his fists and turned away. Stairs to his right led up to a concrete building. He sank down on the bottom step.

That word from before—the one that had come to his lips—rang through his mind. Why was he thinking about his mother? He didn't actually believe that woman was his mom, did he? After all this time, did he really believe she would still turn up?

And yet, he couldn't stop thinking, "What if..."

Overhead, thick clouds slipped past, reflected in the windows of the buildings lining the street. Rachel sat down to Henry's right. She gave him a nudge. "You okay?"

Henry realized how anxious and out-of-sorts he must look. "Yeah," he said.

"Anything you want to talk about?"

"No."

Henry focused on his breathing, trying to let the pain in his chest recede. Rachel put a hand on his shoulder. "Take your time."

As Rachel spoke, her eyes shifted. They narrowed at something behind Henry, back the way they had come. Henry turned.

A thin man, dressed in a black overcoat despite the warmth, strode down the sidewalk toward them. In one hand he held an umbrella, rolled up. In the other, he clutched a briefcase and a yellow sheet of notebook paper.

The man stopped several feet away. He coughed. Rachel's eyes narrowed. "Yeah?"

The man remained still. "You two, I suppose, are the kids who chased that woman?"

A spark shot through Henry. "What about it?"

The man smiled, the corners of his eyes crinkling genially. "Now, now, don't get offended. I come in peace. It's just that…" He set down his briefcase, and then took another step forward. Henry stood, his muscles tensed. "She asked me to give you this."

The man stretched out his hand, offering the folded yellow paper to Henry. Henry stared at the thing in wonder, and then snatched it from the man.

Rachel stood up too. Henry unfolded the paper. Hastily scrawled words, written in that same looping cursive as the note in New York, slanted across the page.

Get back to the investigation. Don't trust all of the neighbors. – S.

Henry turned it over. Nothing on the back. He rubbed his finger across that ornate S. Only one name came to mind—Susan.

Susan Alabaster, his mother. Nobody had ever found out what happened to their plane, after all.

The man started to walk away.

"Wait!"

He turned back, raising his eyebrows. "Yes?"

"Who was she?"

The man shrugged. "Don't know. She handed me a five to give you the note, so I did."

"Well, what did she look like?"

"Middle-aged. Blond hair. Green eyes, or maybe blue, I forget. She was pretty, but nervous."

"You didn't recognize her?"

"She seemed familiar, but I couldn't place her. Sorry."

The man walked away. "Oh, and don't bother looking," he called back over his shoulder. "I'm sure she's long gone by now." He turned down the next street and disappeared from sight.

Henry turned his eyes to the note again. Rachel took a few steps down the sidewalk. "We should go,

Henry. Your uncle is probably looking for us."

Henry took a last look at the note. Then he slipped it into his pocket and followed Rachel. They set off the way they had come.

After a few turns, however, they stopped. None of the bleak buildings and narrow streets surrounding them looked familiar. Had they taken a left or right here? And at the next intersection, should they go straight through, or turn again? Rachel suggested asking for directions, but they didn't remember the name of the restaurant where they'd had brunch. Henry stared up at the alien buildings. He wished Kelvin was there with them now. He'd know the way. He'd always been there for Henry in the past.

No matter. They'd eaten brunch near the boardwalk, Henry knew, and they could definitely find the shore, then work their way back from there. With this plan in mind, he and Rachel set off, and soon the welcome roar of water met their ears and the vast ocean stretched in the distance.

But it was not a familiar sight. This was not the same place they'd seen from the restaurant. No boardwalk lined the water here, and the crowds of laughing and walking people had been replaced by a few stragglers with binoculars and kites.

And, beyond the people, a great structure stood near a distant pier, framed by the turbid blue of the ocean and the increasingly gray sky. Banded with narrow, alternating rings of black and white, the Sandy Run lighthouse loomed over the breaking waves of the sea.

Chapter Fourteen

The Sandy Run Lighthouse

Even from a distance, the Sandy Run lighthouse dominated the landscape. Seagulls circled near its top, and more dotted the flat, grassy land at its moss-covered base, flapping and stretching their wings.

Somehow, the lighthouse appeared solemn and mysterious, as if it was hinting at all the unexplored places in the world, all the undiscovered secrets waiting to be found.

Rachel started forward. "If we go to the top," she suggested, "maybe we can see our way back."

They jogged toward the grassy area surrounding the lighthouse. A wooden booth sat at the edge of the grass. Mounted on its side was a sign that read *Lighthouse admission: free*. A gaunt man with a long beard leaned out of the booth as they passed.

"Headin' to the lighthouse?"

Henry stopped. "Yeah."

The man eyed the two of them. He had the weathered look of an old sailor. "No adults?"

Rachel shook her head. "No."

The man flattened his long gray mustache between his thin fingers, studying Henry and Rachel. He turned his eyes toward the lighthouse. "She's a beaut', ain't she?"

"Sure," Henry replied, "it's really cool."

Quick as could be, the man whipped his head back around to them, a joyful glint in his eyes. "There are folks here who say she's too big, you know? Hogwash, says I. They say she blocks the view. Well ain't that just the most foolish thing you ever heard? She *is* the view."

Rachel stared at the lighthouse. It towered against the sky. "I think you're right."

The man studied them again, twisting an end of his mustache. Raising an overgrown eyebrow, he glanced at the dark clouds overhead, then back at Henry and Rachel. "Well, don't be long," he said. "Weather's getting nasty. Fifteen minutes, or I'm comin' up after you."

Rachel gave a quick, "Thanks!" and she and Henry started across the grass. The wind picked up, tossing Rachel's ponytail around and billowing Henry's shirt. Beyond the huge shape of the lighthouse, only small patches of blue showed between fast-moving clouds. A large wave crashed against the nearby pier, shooting up a spray of white mist. Seagulls flew into the air, squawking in irritation.

Grabbing the handle of the old lighthouse, Rachel pulled. The splintered door came open with a long, uneasy creak. Inside, metal steps led in a tight spiral into the darkness above.

"After you," Rachel said.

Henry stepped inside. The door blew shut behind them, muffling the howl of the wind and extinguishing all of the light except for that coming from a few weak bulbs and slit-like windows. The stairs made a dull metallic clang with each step as Henry and Rachel ascended.

After what felt like several minutes, a bright hole appeared above them. Henry emerged into a small, circular room with glass walls. He helped Rachel up. Through the walls, he saw a balcony wrapping around the lighthouse. Beyond, the vast ocean stretched away beneath swirling gray clouds.

"Look at this, Henry," Rachel said.

A metal platform stood in the center of the room, topped by something that looked like a huge glass cocoon. Not a cocoon for any sort of insect, though. It was a cocoon, Henry realized, for a lantern.

"It's a Fresnel lens," Rachel said. She turned to Henry. "Like, a magnifying glass, you know? It's what lets you see the light way out at sea. We're right at the heart of the lighthouse."

Henry nodded. But instead of looking at the

lens, he looked at Rachel. When they'd first met in the hotel two nights ago, he had noticed her headstrong attitude. He had admired it, but now, as he watched her marvel at the Fresnel lens, he realized he hadn't given her enough credit. Underneath her fierce determination, she was brilliant and inquisitive too.

It seemed, Henry realized with a smile, that she just didn't like to show it.

"Why're you gawking at me, Henry?"

"No reason."

Rachel rolled her eyes and turned away. A set of stairs led up to the lantern, but a locked gate blocked the way. *Closed to the public*, read a sign. Rachel shook the gate, but it rattled without opening. Henry spotted a door on the outer wall. As he pulled it open, a gust of wind swirled into the room.

Henry stepped out onto the balcony, taking a deep breath of salty air. Out there before him, spanning to the horizon under the mottled gray sky, lay the ocean.

Rachel followed him out and they leaned against the railing together. Gusty wind topped the ocean waves with white spray. Far out there, miles and miles away, a few big ships slowly churned their way out to sea.

Rachel gave him a bump on the arm. "Don't look down."

Henry looked down.

She was right. He shouldn't have. His head swirled at the distance to the ground. He gripped the railing with white knuckles and gave her a dirty look.

"I told you not to. Come on. Let's see if we can spot the boardwalk."

They followed the metal balcony to the far side of the lighthouse. Sure enough, the boardwalk stretched away to the north. To the west stood the assorted buildings of Sandy Run.

Beyond those buildings hung a dark sky, swelling with storm clouds.

These were behemoth storm clouds, too—great gray and white cumulonimbus in the distance, stretching like mountains of ink-blotted whipped cream to the north and south. At the top of the mammoth clouds, a thin shelf stretched out in advance of the bulk. At the bottom, rain tumbled out in distant patches, falling to the ground somewhere beyond the buildings of the town. Several smaller clouds hung in front of the main ones, looking like tiny strands of cotton before a huge mass of white and gray.

"Well, you said it was going to storm, didn't you?" Rachel made a sweeping gesture with her hand, smiling widely. "There you go."

Henry grinned too. The wind, gusty and uneven, blustered through their clothes and hair, bringing a sense of exhilaration as they stood watching the huge clouds roll slowly closer.

Rachel leaned forward, her elbows on the railing. "So those are cumulonimbus clouds, right?"

"Yeah," Henry replied. The huge clouds looked just like the ones in the books in Kelvin's study. More than once, Henry and Kelvin had paged through those books together on stormy nights, looking at pictures of clouds as thunderclaps rattled the living room window. The clouds looked a bit like huge anvils, with wide flat tops reaching out ahead of the bulk.

"Those things can get about seven miles tall," Henry said.

Rachel stared. "Seven miles?"

"Yeah. When a cloud gets about that tall it hits the bottom of the, uh, what did Kelvin call it... stratosphere. It can't really go higher than that, so it spreads out."

Henry smiled as he spoke, glad they weren't underneath it yet. He had seen this type of cloud before, but usually from underneath. That was a very wet place to be. The lighthouse offered an ideal view.

Rachel shifted her weight, looking more pensive. "Edward Wrightly died in a storm like this, huh?"

"Yeah, something like this."

"Too bad. I never paid much attention to storms before. Just enough to be inside when one comes,

149

you know? But you probably know a bunch about them, right? With your uncle and all."

Henry gave a shrug, but he couldn't deny it. As much as it surprised him, he did remember a lot of what Kelvin had taught him over the past months. A lot of it was really pretty cool.

Rachel motioned out over the railing. Somehow it felt as if they were standing at the top of the world, with all of the earth laid out before them. "So what about this storm? Tell me something about it. How's it work?"

"How's it work?"

"Yeah. If we were chefs, what would we need to cook up a storm like this?"

Henry leaned on the railing too. The warmth of Rachel's shoulder against his own helped him ignore the dizzying drop to the ground below. Remembering what Kelvin had once told him, he began slowly.

"Well, the ingredients for making a storm are the same as for making a normal cloud, for the most part. So, ingredient one: enough water vapor— that's evaporated water—near the ground. Clouds are made of water, and it's hard to make one if you just don't have much."

Rachel nodded. "That's why deserts don't have many clouds."

"Right. So, uh, ingredient two: the atmosphere needs to get cold pretty quickly as you go up. Warm air rises, and if the air at the ground is too cold compared to the air above it, it's hard to make it go up. That's why we get more storms in the summer. It's usually warmer and more humid."

In the distance, the dark whipped-cream storm slowly heaped up on itself, looking like a series of dollops on the top of some colossal pumpkin pie. "All right, water vapor and warm air," Rachel said. "Anything else?"

"Just one more thing. We need to give the air a push."

"A push?"

"Sure, as long as we have the other things, air will keep going up. But, unless it's really hot, we need something to get it going."

Rachel looked doubtful. "So how do we do that?"

"There are a couple of ways, I think. If it's warm enough, air can rise on its own. It does that in summer a lot. But it can also, let's see, come together with other air and go up, go over a mountain, or... what was the last one? Oh yeah, it can be lifted by a front. Fronts are when cold air and warm air meet. The warm air goes up over the cold air because warm air is lighter. That's what's causing this storm."

Digging into his pocket, Henry pulled out his barometer. Under the glass, the needle pointed even farther to the left. That end of the dial bore a single word: rain.

Henry tapped on the word. "Storms and rain usually happen near low pressure. Lows have rising air, so rough weather is more likely. And fronts are more likely near low pressure too."

As he held the barometer, Henry felt a lot like his uncle. It was an odd sensation. He felt as if he should be wearing a detective hat and coat.

Out in front of them, the storm crept closer. Rachel asked, "So if we have those ingredients, we can make a cloud?"

Henry nodded, glad she didn't want to leave yet. "Yeah. The air goes up. Once it's high enough, the water vapor starts to condense into a cloud. It's really cold up there, and cold air can't keep as much water vapor, so it has to turn into tiny droplets of water or ice. That's what clouds are made of. Water

and ice."

"So why don't they fall?"

"They try to fall, but the pieces are just so small that the rising air can keep them up. If there are enough little pieces, though, they start to stick together and get bigger."

Rachel understood immediately. "And if they get big enough, they fall out of the cloud as snow or rain."

"Yeah." Henry motioned out at the storm. "Really, the only difference between a normal cloud and something like this is the strength of the ingredients. Add stronger ingredients and instead of a little white cloud you get something huge like this."

He and Rachel both looked at that great storm creeping toward them, dark and impressive, an awesome show of nature. That huge anvil head on top stretched out above them now, sliding along the bottom of the stratosphere, seven miles up. Henry wished they could stay on the lighthouse all day.

"It's pretty amazing," Rachel said with a sigh. She looked at him. "Just one more question."

"Yeah?"

"Why do we get hail?"

The question gave Henry an uneasy jolt. The wind gusted between him and Rachel. Henry thought about poor Ed Wrightly, coming home in the hailstorm and being murdered. He clenched the railing in his hand, letting his eyes drop from the cloud to the street at the edge of town below. What a terrible, vile thing to happen.

"Hail," he explained, "is different from rain or snow. In a big storm, air goes up so fast that small things like snowflakes can't fall down..."

Something on the distant street caught Henry's eye. His words trailed off. A man down there, far away, had crept to the corner of an alley and paused. From here he looked no larger than an ant.

Henry shook his head. "Instead of falling," he went on, "ice gets pushed higher into the cloud, then falls a little, then gets pushed back up. Each time the pieces do this, more ice freezes onto them and they grow."

The tiny figure below started to walk. Henry squinted. The man held two things in his hands. One looked long and black, possibly an umbrella. The other, Henry realized, was a baseball bat.

Rodger Salmon. What was he doing out here?

"And when the ice gets heavy enough," Rachel said, finishing Henry's thought, "it comes crashing back to earth."

Crack. Henry imagined the blow to the back of Mr. Wrightly's head. The killing stroke. Not from a hailstone, but from something else.

As he watched Rodger Salmon hurry off down the street, he couldn't help picturing the powerful, violent swing of a baseball bat.

Chapter Fifteen

The Storm

A sudden flash of light came from within the belly of the storm, illuminating the dark clouds. The shadowy band of rain, previously a thin strip of darkness far away, now threatened to swallow them.

Henry glanced back to the street. Rodger Salmon was gone. The wind picked up, slamming against Henry and Rachel. The sky hung darkly overhead. Exactly five seconds after the flash, a shuddering, deafening crack of thunder blasted over them.

At that second, Henry realized a lighthouse wasn't the best place to be in a thunderstorm.

"Hey!" A faint shout rose on the wind from the ground below. The old sailor ran across the grass toward the lighthouse, waving his arms. He and the seagulls below all looked very, very small. "Hey, get down!"

Rachel and Henry didn't argue. Whipping

around, they ran back though the glass room with its complex cocoon and down the dizzying set of dark stairs. A few seconds later, heads spinning, they pushed out into the blustery air again.

Behind them, wind slammed the door shut.

"I told you fifteen minutes!"

"Sorry."

The old sailor's cheeks flushed red. "It's okay, but get on out of here. It's about to start dumping cats and dogs."

Rachel nodded. She and Henry tore across the grassy lawn at full speed.

Abruptly, the wind changed direction and grew colder.

The edge of the cold front, the exact thing that caused all those huge clouds, had just passed over them. With it would come the rain—the cats and dogs, yowling on their way down.

"We shouldn't have stayed so long!" Rachel yelled, still running.

A cold drop smacked Henry on the forehead and ran into his eye. He thought about Rodger Salmon. "Yeah, you're right."

More large raindrops streaked down. Above, the edge of the darker clouds crept over them like some colossal UFO. Henry and Rachel flew past the wooden booth, heading toward the street where Rodger Salmon had been moments before. Shops and restaurants lined the road, and a large blue and white awning stretched over the sidewalk on the far side. Beyond the buildings hung a dark sky, thick with rain.

Another flash of light. Two seconds later, a crash of thunder. It cracked more loudly this time, echoing off buildings. Hands above their heads, Henry and Rachel reached the awning just as the air behind became a torrent of water.

Rachel leaned against the wall, catching her breath. "That was close!"

Elsewhere on the street, a few unfortunate people still ran for cover, hands or newspapers above their heads. The lighthouse remained visible in the distance for a few seconds, but the rain soon enveloped it in gray sheets of water.

Where was Rodger Salmon? Henry looked around. Rodger wasn't in sight.

"What now?" Rachel asked.

"I saw someone. Rodger Salmon, the guy who argued with his wife in the alley yesterday. I don't know why he was here, but he looked suspicious."

Rachel became more alert. "Where?"

"Not sure. This way, I think. Come on."

They started jogging north under the awning. An intersection lay ahead. Heavy sheets of rain tossed back and forth in the open street.

"Which way?" Rachel asked.

"Straight on, I guess."

On the count of three, they ran.

In the distance, a flash illuminated the deep clouds. It lit up the rain, which pummeled Henry and Rachel in swirling curtains. They leapt under the awning on the far side, thoroughly soaked. The crash of thunder echoed around them, like boulders cracking together in a rockslide.

"Sort of dangerous out here," Henry said.

Rachel wiped the rain from her dark hair. "We'll have to chance it. I don't want to stay here. Come on."

They kept walking. Henry looked around, scanning through the downpour for the tall man with the baseball bat. Rachel peered into shops. An awful, creeping sensation stole over Henry— a feeling that Rodger Salmon could jump from around a corner at any moment, swinging his bat. Maybe they shouldn't be out here.

Henry stopped. Farther along, on the oceanfront side of the street, stood an outdoor bar. Something about it jogged Henry's memory. Water poured through the fake grass roof above the bar, splattering onto barstools. Fat raindrops bounced off the surrounding tables, the tall umbrellas in their centers rolled up and fluttering. In front, an anchor read *The Mariner's Draught.* Underneath: *Closed for storm repair.*

The Mariner's Draught. Henry had heard that name before, but where? Darn it, he couldn't remember!

Rachel grabbed his arm. "Look."

She pointed farther down their side of the road, across the next intersection. Through the rain, Henry saw a man standing on the far street corner, dark umbrella in hand. He was staring at the bar too. He stamped his foot and seemed to curse, though Henry couldn't hear anything over the howling wind and spattering rain. The man turned and began to stomp back across the intersection toward Henry and Rachel, a baseball bat gripped in his left hand.

Henry recognized him for certain this time. Rodger Salmon.

"Quick," Rachel hissed, "hide." She pulled Henry's arm and dragged him to a store entrance, yanking the handle. Locked. They were trapped. "Just pretend to look inside, okay? Did he spot us?"

Henry followed her example, pressing his face to the glass, trying to look innocuous. "I don't think so," he hissed back.

Rodger trudged past them, cursing quietly. Henry held his breath. He thought he noticed a glance in their direction. Rodger cursed again, quickened his pace, and disappeared around the next corner.

"Did he see us?" Rachel asked.

"I think so."

Henry looked across the street again. "Something about the bar upset him."

"The Mariner's Draught," Rachel read.

Henry started. "That's it! That's the bar Rodger said he stayed at on the night of the storm. Just look at it! It's all torn up."

Rachel's eyes widened. "He lied. There's no way he hung out there in a hailstorm." She looked at the corner where Rodger had disappeared. "Want to see where he went?"

Henry nodded. They crept forward and peered around the edge of the dark bricks. About a block away, Rodger stood by himself. A small light illuminated the side of his face. A cell phone.

Rodger looked to be talking with someone. After a few seconds, he shut his phone and started walking again, disappearing down a wet alleyway.

Rachel glanced at Henry, but the next words didn't come from her. They came from behind Henry.

"Spying on someone, are we?"

Henry just about jumped out of his shoes. He spun around, ready to defend himself.

But he didn't have to.

Standing there in his long tan coat and floppy hat, large umbrella in hand, was someone Henry definitely wanted to see.

"Kelvin!"

"Henry!"

Rachel clutched her chest. She stamped her foot. "You just about gave me a heart attack,

The Storm

Mr. McCloud!"

Henry gave Kelvin a big wet hug. "How'd you find us, Kelvin?"

Kelvin grinned and replied, "What kind of detective would I be if I couldn't find my own assistants?"

Chapter Sixteen

Detective Work

As Henry released his uncle, Kelvin looked down at his coat. On top of the faint white image of a cat, he now had a large Henry-shaped wet spot. He frowned. "You two are soaked."

It was true—Henry and Rachel's clothes sagged and their hair dripped. Before Henry could say anything, however, Kelvin gripped him by both shoulders and looked him straight in the eyes. "And you shouldn't have run off." Kelvin glanced at Rachel. "Either of you. Your parents and I have been sick with worry. We're chasing a murderer here, and I can't keep you two safe if I don't know where you are."

Henry stared back. "But it was the woman from New York," he said. "She was here."

"Regardless, you shouldn't run off."

Henry glanced at his feet. His dripping started to form a puddle on the concrete. He didn't know what else to say.

"Did you see who was just here, Mr. McCloud?" Rachel asked.

Kelvin stared at Henry for a moment more, then released his shoulders. He stepped to the corner and peeked around it. "I did. Rodger Salmon."

After a second's hesitation, Henry stepped up beside his uncle and peered around the corner as well. The street stood empty, gusting with rain. "We think he's up to something. His alibi was a lie."

Kelvin looked back at Henry. "Oh?"

"He said he was at the Mariner's Draught that night. It's an outdoor bar."

"It's all torn up from the storm," Rachel said.

Kelvin narrowed his eyes. "I see. In that case, we need to find out where Mr. Salmon is swimming in all this rain."

A pulse of excitement jolted through Henry. "You want to follow him?"

"Yes. And you two will be safer with me than on your own. Just stay close, okay?"

They slipped around the corner. The awning ended, but Henry and Rachel stayed under Kelvin's large umbrella, which took the brunt of the swirling, pounding rain.

Kelvin put his phone to his ear.

"Yes, Clarence, I've found them. No, no, they're fine. We'll meet you back at the car in half an hour."

He hung up. On the far side of the street, they

approached the empty alleyway Rodger had fled down.

"This is the one," Rachel said with a nod.

"Then let's hurry," Kelvin said. They jogged past wet trashcans and over puddles in the alleyway. Rain streamed down the brick walls to their sides.

Kelvin held up a hand. They crept to a halt, peering into the next street. The rain swirled and splattered against their faces, making it difficult to see.

"There!" Henry said. About a hundred feet down the road stood Rodger Salmon, umbrella in hand.

"Good," said Kelvin. "Let's watch."

Rachel nodded.

Rodger peered around himself. Kelvin leaned his umbrella back into the alleyway, out of sight. After a moment, Rodger began moving again, disappearing down another street.

They started to jog. Henry noticed his uncle smiling. "I was here yesterday morning, you know," Kelvin said.

Henry tried to stay under the umbrella. "What does that matter?"

"Because I think I know where he's going. The only question is why."

They reached the next corner and stopped again. A much wider street lay beyond, lined with lit streetlights, businesses, and shops. Henry caught sight of Rodger jogging up a set of concrete steps. Pushing through a revolving glass door, the tall man disappeared into a bank.

Henry checked the sign out front. *The Oceanside Banking and Loan*. The very place the dead man had worked.

Rachel put her hand to her mouth. Above, the dark clouds illuminated with a flash.

Of all the places in Sandy Run, why had Rodger Salmon come here?

Henry stopped himself. Maybe Rodger came here to cash some checks, he reasoned. After all, the dreariness and ferocity of thunderstorms made even the most ordinary activities seem sinister.

"We've got to see what he's up to," Rachel said.

Kelvin nodded. "Yes, we do." He looked at them both. "And don't worry. There are lots of cameras and guards in a bank. Nothing bad will happen."

Running through the rain, they ascended the bank's concrete steps, slick with water. The lobby cast light into the rain through large windows. Henry couldn't see Rodger inside. He pushed through the revolving glass door, Kelvin and Rachel close behind.

"Here." Kelvin tossed Rachel a small cloth from inside his coat. She dried her face, and then Henry did the same. When he looked back up, Rachel and Kelvin were already scanning the empty lobby.

Rachel squeezed her lips together in frustration. "Man, where'd he go?"

At the far side of the lobby, two bankers in dark suits stood behind counters. Kelvin wasn't looking at the bankers, though. He was looking at the floor. Wet footprints led off to the left.

They started walking again, careful to look inconspicuous. The tracks led to a hallway off the main lobby, where the employee offices lined a wall. Mr. Wrightly's old office stood at the very end, his nameplate still mounted beside the large oak door.

The footprints soon disappeared on the hallway's carpet, but Henry, Rachel, and Kelvin kept going. They headed for the end of the hall.

Why would Rodger come to Edward Wrightly's old office? To steal? To cover up evidence? The door stood closed and forbidding. The three of them stopped at the end of the hall, listening.

No sounds emanated from the other side of the door. No talking, no rustling, no anything. They waited a moment, but nothing changed. Kelvin's mouth curled in frustration.

Henry tried the door. Locked. It would have been locked for Rodger, too.

"How'd he even get in?" Rachel whispered.

Abruptly, Kelvin turned and paced back down the hall, stopping at a different door. He winked to Henry and Rachel. They followed, and this time they did hear something. On the other side of the door, a man and a woman argued in hushed voices.

Henry glanced at the nameplate beside the door.

Mrs. Victoria Sharp. Of course! How could Henry forget that she worked here too?

Scarcely wanting to breathe, he listened.

"Calm down, Rodger, you're blowing this out of proportion. Just sit down and we'll sort this out."

Muffled through the door, Rodger's voice moved from side to side, accompanied by footsteps. "Sort it out? We both know I messed up. And now Elena knows too. I was at The Mariner's Draught just now. I'm such an idiot! It's all outdoors. She must have called them that night. That's how she found out."

"She's your wife. Of course she was going to find out sooner or later. You can't hide things like this from her."

Rodger's voice continued in a low groan. "I know. But it was my mistake. I wanted to fix it. Oh, how'd I get into this mess? With that detective digging around, soon everybody will know. I just don't see a way out of it."

"Look, sit down. I'll help you. And we'll keep it between us. Nobody else needs to know."

A soft noise came from behind Henry. He turned around. A banker stood at the entrance to the hallway, her arms crossed, giving them a severe look.

Kelvin saw the banker too. Straightening up, he offered an apologetic smile. "Sorry. Just making sure my friend is here. Need to talk with her."

Saying this, he gave the door a few loud raps with his knuckle.

Inside, the voices stopped. A few seconds passed in silence. A woman called out through the door, sweetly.

"Who is it?"

"Kelvin McCloud. We spoke yesterday, Mrs. Sharp. I was hoping I could ask you some questions."

Another few seconds of silence, then faint whispers. The door swung open and a red-faced Rodger Salmon rushed out. He bumped past Kelvin, making for the lobby. Henry again noticed his hefty baseball bat and those hailstone welts on his arms and legs.

Henry wanted to go after him, but Kelvin gave a subtle shake of the head. Rodger slipped from sight. Henry heard the lobby door revolving.

Victoria came to her office door, her fiery red hair tied up in a tight bun. She wore a business suit, and a set of small, circular glasses rested on her nose. She managed a brief, stern smile.

"Ah, the detective. How nice."

"Hello again, Mrs. Sharp," Kelvin replied. "May we come in?"

Victoria stepped back, motioning with a thin arm for them to enter. "Now that you've interrupted things with my client, of course, feel free."

Henry ignored the tinge of venom in Victoria's voice. Before stepping forward, he noticed the large wet spots he and Rachel had made on the hallway carpet. As he passed into the office, he shrugged to the banker at the far end of the hall.

Victoria shut the door with a clear metallic click. On the far wall, white blinds covered most of a large window, leaving only a small gap. Howling wind and rain pummeled the far side, battering the thick glass.

"Sit, please," Victoria said. She gestured at a line of chairs, and then sat down opposite them at her polished maple desk. Her eyes remained focused and cold. "What may I assist you with?"

Kelvin sat down, crossed one leg over the other, and set his dripping umbrella on the floor. He motioned to the door. "Whispered conversations behind closed doors can't help but look suspicious the week after your boss died, you know."

Victoria's expression remained unchanged. "Your point being?"

Kelvin shrugged. He had dropped his overenthusiastic act. "We'll get back to that later. For now, I'd like you to explain something to me. It's something that's been puzzling me. The teenagers."

A slight pause. "The teenagers?"

Kelvin gave a curt nod. "Correct. The last time we spoke, you insisted to me there were no teenagers at Mr. Wrightly's mansion on the nights after the storm."

"Yes, that's accurate."

"But you are lying to us."

Victoria straightened herself up, a fierce intensity coming into her eyes. "Is that what this is about? This teenager business again, Mr. McCloud?"

Henry was curious too. What about Rodger Salmon? Still, his uncle must have a good reason to save that for later. Feeling he should say something, Henry added, "Frank Rosenbloom said the teens were definitely there those nights."

"Frank Rosenbloom? What would he know?"

Rachel leaned forward. "He insisted. He told us a light came on in your house at two a.m. on the second night."

A hint of crimson came into Victoria's cheeks, but she remained seated. "Then it's slander. No light came on. He's inventing tales to incriminate us."

"Us?" Rachel asked.

"Ahem, I mean me. The royal 'us'."

Kelvin held up his palms. "As it happens, Mrs. Sharp, it doesn't really matter if a light in your house came on or not. We ran into one of the teens yesterday. He was inside the mansion, stealing."

Victoria didn't respond immediately. For the tiniest fraction of a second, her eyes flicked down to a dust-free spot on the corner of her desk.

"I assure you, Mr. McCloud, I have no idea what you're talking about."

"I think you do. The boy ran from me, arms full of silver dishes. He knew his way around the place, too, or else he wouldn't have escaped. It wasn't his first time there. Now why did you lie?"

Victoria tightened her lips and gave Kelvin a venomous glare, but didn't respond. Kelvin glared back at her.

Left out of this staring contest, Henry looked at the corner of Victoria's desk. The dust-free spot where she had glanced had a distinct shape. It looked like a thin rectangle about six inches long, with a short line poking out the nearer long side. What had been sitting there?

Henry looked elsewhere. Along one wall ran a shelf of books about banking rules and regulations. Next to these sat a plant, and next to that stood a yellow and blue porcelain bird.

Henry kept looking. The splatter of rain and dull rumblings of thunder washed against the closed window. Henry saw no latch in the gap between the curtains. It wasn't the sort of window that opened.

Rachel pointed to the dust-free spot on the desk. "Mrs. Sharp, did a picture frame used to sit here?"

Victoria's eyes shot at Rachel. She opened her mouth, closed it, and then abruptly laughed. "Ah, yes, so there was. A picture of my dog, Poochie. I thought the place needed some freshening up, so I retired it. But will that be all, Mr. McCloud?"

Enough. This had gone on too long. "Mrs. Sharp,"

Henry said, "we heard you and Rodger talking through the door. Tell us the truth. Rodger murdered your boss, didn't he?"

Victoria jumped. "What? Murdered?" She looked between the three of them rapidly. "Why, I... Ed was murdered? I had no idea."

"So you claim," Henry snapped back.

Henry felt Kelvin's hand on his shoulder and turned. Kelvin shook his head. "Slow down Henry. Remember, evidence before conclusions."

Henry gaped. "But we heard them through the door. They were trying to cover something up."

"And Rodger and his wife were bickering in the alley yesterday," Rachel said. "He'd done something terrible."

"Plus," Henry went on, "what about the baseball bat?"

Victoria shook her head. "He plays baseball, child."

"But it would've made the perfect weapon, you have to admit."

Kelvin nodded. "Perhaps. But you're jumping to conclusions, Henry. You've presented some evidence, and constructed a theory, but you have to be careful. Theories have to agree with all of the evidence, not just some of it. You can't just ignore evidence that disproves your idea."

"What?" Henry asked. "What did I leave out?"

Kelvin tapped his notebook with a pen. "For one,

remember what I told you at brunch. One of Mrs. Sharp's coworkers was here, working late on the night of the murder. A man came in to see Victoria around eight, and didn't leave until several hours later, leaving through the hail. He was tall, and talking about baseball. I should have figured this out much sooner, but I only pieced it together when I saw that same man come here today."

Henry's eyes widened. "Rodger Salmon."

"So Rodger was here when Mr. Wrightly died?" Rachel asked.

Victoria straightened her back and interlaced her thin fingers. "That's correct. Perhaps now you'll think a little before accusing someone of murder."

Henry gritted his teeth. "But why was he here?" he asked. "Why come to the bank in the middle of a hailstorm?"

Kelvin leaned back. "Well, I know some of the story. The other employee said that Rodger was ranting about losing his savings gambling on baseball. Gambling can be a terrible addiction, and losing a lot of money can be an embarrassment to anyone. So why come to a bank? I suspect Rodger was looking for financial advice. He probably didn't want anyone else to know, so he arranged to meet Victoria during the hailstorm when he didn't expect others to be here. Maybe not the best plan, but sometimes emotional people don't make the best decisions." Kelvin cast his eyes up at Victoria. "Is that correct?"

She adjusted her bun of fiery red hair. "You've got the gist of it, Mr. McCloud. Rodger is a very proud man when it comes to sports. I promised him I wouldn't tell anyone, but you seem to have figured out most everything already. Besides, if the alternative is being accused of murder"—she cast her cold eyes at Henry—"then I guess it's better to let you know what actually happened. I'd ask that you not to spread the news any further, however."

Henry sat quiet for a moment, trying to process this information. A lousy gambling addiction? That was really what all this business with Rodger Salmon was about? The reason for the lies and secrecy? The fight in the alleyway? That was why Mrs. Salmon stormed out of the book club?

A sinking feeling grew in Henry's stomach. It all made sense, but unlike most puzzles, this wasn't the slightest bit satisfying to solve. Just when it seemed that their investigation sat on the verge of a breakthrough, most of their leads had suddenly dried up.

"So this doesn't have to do with Mr. Wrightly's death at all?" Henry asked.

Kelvin looked at him with a thin smile. "No, nothing at all. You'll find, Henry, that most people have secrets. People have embarrassments and insecurities, and things they don't want others to know. Most of these secrets aren't illegal, and most of them aren't even really wrong. But it's our job to find the ones that are." He shot his eyes back over to Victoria. "Speaking of which, I still want to know your secret, Mrs. Sharp. Why are you lying to us about the teenagers?"

Victoria nudged her circular glasses farther up her nose. "Like I told you before, Mr. McCloud, there were no teenagers." She hesitated, then added, "And even if there were, they didn't have anything to do with the death."

On this point she would say nothing more. She maintained her straight-backed posture behind her large maple desk, her fingers still interlocked on its surface.

Kelvin shook his head. "Fine, keep your secret. We'll find out some other way." He looked through his notes. "There are some other questions I'd like to ask you about the night of the murder, though."

"Ask away."

"First: when, precisely, did Edward leave work?"

Victoria considered the question. "He left around nine, I think. Yes, nine exactly."

"And how long is the drive back to your neighborhood?"

"Fifteen minutes."

Henry considered this. Assuming no stops or delays, and assuming Victoria was telling the truth, Ed Wrightly would have gotten home at nine fifteen, right when Frank Rosenbloom saw the car go up the driveway. Only minutes before, Frank had seen the flickering light from the fire.

"Why'd Edward leave work so late, anyway?" Rachel asked.

Victoria raised her eyebrows. "Late, young lady? No, Edward obsessed over his job. He rarely left before midnight, and only left on the night of the storm to make sure hail wasn't breaking his windows. I'm surprised nobody told you all this, but Edward wasn't leaving late that night. He was leaving early."

Chapter Seventeen

Dinner and Stories

As the storm outside continued to thrash against the window, Henry, Rachel, and Kelvin posed further questions. They wanted to hear everything, to the letter, that Victoria knew about her boss's untimely demise.

First, what could she tell them about the threatening letters in Edward Wrightly's study? Unfortunately, not much. She simply recalled a period, a few months after Edward built the new manor, when he suddenly stopped bragging about the place. He seemed thoroughly distraught about something. It occurred very close to this time last year.

Second, where was Victoria's husband, Walter, on the night of the murder? At home, Victoria insisted, with their son.

Finally, Henry asked about Victoria's neighbors. Victoria rolled a pen between her fingers as she answered.

"We don't see each other very much anymore, to tell the truth. The last time we all got together was for breakfast at Isabel and Eugene's house, probably two years ago. I didn't enjoy myself. It was cloudy that morning, and Eugene always got a little ornery when something blocked his view of the sunrise. He was being most unpleasant. Frank Rosenbloom, too. He wouldn't stop talking about something-or-other at work." She shrugged. "Like I said, I don't really see them much anymore."

The clock on the wall read ten minutes after five o'clock. Standing, Kelvin thanked Victoria and led Henry and Rachel out of the banker's office. Pushing out through the revolving glass door, they returned to the squall.

Henry sloshed through puddles in the road. "Well that was a waste of time."

Kelvin held his large umbrella at a steep angle, pushing against the wind. "What do you mean?"

Rachel replied for him. "We didn't learn much."

Kelvin shrugged, seeming more satisfied than Henry expected. "I wouldn't say that. For one, we now know who didn't do it. Learning anything, even if it isn't what you set out to find, can be helpful. If we keep narrowing it down, we'll know the answer in no time."

Henry hadn't thought about it like that before—the process of elimination. It could be useful in a pinch, to narrow things down. Maybe his uncle had a point.

A crack of thunder rumbled off the sides of rain-soaked buildings. Kelvin led the way down unfamiliar streets until the restaurant from brunch came back into sight and, beyond it, Kelvin's car.

Two figures emerged from the vehicle, opening umbrellas.

"Rachel!" Vanessa cried out, jogging through the rain toward them. "Where on earth have you been? You scared us half to death, running off like that!"

"Sorry, Mom." Rachel rubbed the back of her neck. "I didn't think you'd notice." Vanessa wrapped her in a fierce hug.

Behind Vanessa, the rounder figure of Clarence Willowby waddled through the rain.

"Are you hurt?" he called out.

Rachel struggled to remove her face from her mother's shoulder. "No, Dad," she called back. "We're fine."

Following this came a fair amount of motherly looking-over-for-bruises, a small lecture with scolding and finger-wagging from Dad, and a whole lot of Rachel explaining to them why she ran off and telling them not to worry, she was a big girl now, thanks all the same.

Henry, standing quietly beside his uncle in the rain, only watched.

At last the Willowbys broke ranks. Clarence

strode over to Henry and Kelvin, patting himself on his belly. "Well I'm starved. How about back the hotel for a change of clothes, then out to dinner?"

Before the hour was out, they all sat down in a dark and warm steakhouse, dry clothes upon their backs and pleasant sounds and savory smells thick in the air. A real fireplace puffed and squelched nearby, reacting to the wind gusting by the top of the chimney, but it still cast light and heat into the dining room. Henry leaned back, soaking it up. Finally, a bit of warmth and safety.

As dinner came, a variety of enjoyable conversations took place, including a number of stories and jokes from a progressively more cheerful, more red-faced Clarence Willowby, and the howl of stormy weather outside was mostly ignored, replaced by warmer, drier thoughts.

"Oh, India was great," Clarence told them, motioning with a rib bone as he recounted past business trips. "That was years ago. Company sent me over there for Christmas to work on some accounts. Busy time for me, but they have such great spices in their foods that I didn't complain. We could stand to use some of that over here in America. Course, Rachel was too young for that one." He gave Rachel a nudge. "But you remember Australia, don't you, darling?"

Rachel nodded, smiling, and said, "Of course. You should've been there, Henry. The culture was awesome, and you can get boomerangs at, like, every other store!"

"Kangaroos, too," Clarence interjected. "Loads of 'em."

"Clarence and I had to do a bit of work," Vanessa added.

"But we saw 'em from the window!" Clarence finished. He hiccupped, and then turned his wobbly head toward Kelvin. "We went last January. Got on the plane in winter but got off it in summer. Still January, though! That gave me a kick. Good thing I brought my swim trunks."

Rachel poured steak sauce over her sirloin. "I bet you know all about that, right, Mr. McCloud? How the seasons are opposite down there?"

"Sure do."

"Then out with it, professor!" Vanessa said with a hearty laugh. "Teach us about it."

Henry hid a grin. Vanessa hadn't meant anything by it, but she had called his uncle 'professor'. Kelvin still loved to teach, that much was clear, but he rarely spoke about his old job at the university anymore. Only once or twice, late at night, did Henry overhear Kelvin muttering something about a Dr. Ravenhorst, though he could never pry any more information from his uncle.

But oh well. Such were the mysteries of life. As long as they didn't hurt anyone, Henry couldn't see the harm in a few secrets. As Kelvin had said, everyone has secrets. Besides, Henry was confident that, sooner or later, Kelvin would tell him about it on his own.

To Henry's side, Kelvin did a good job masking his eagerness about the seasons question. Professor or not, he was always ready to teach. Taking a roll from the basket at the center of the table, he skewered it, from top to bottom, with a toothpick.

"All right, imagine this roll is Earth. The ends of the toothpick are the North and South Poles." Kelvin frowned, brushing away a few crumbs. "Earth isn't as flaky as this."

"Or as edible!" Clarence interjected with a raucous laugh.

"But it'll do." Kelvin slid the table's candle closer to himself, the light flickering up onto his genial features and hawkish nose. "Now pretend our candle here is the sun. The earth is tilted a bit to the side—23.5 degrees, to be more precise—and revolves around the sun once per year. That's how the year is defined. Since the earth is tilted, part of the year the Northern Hemisphere is getting more direct sunlight, and part of the year the Southern Hemisphere is getting more direct sunlight."

Kelvin began moving the roll in a large, slow circle around the candle. At first the top half was more illuminated by the candle. As it revolved to the other side, the bottom half became better lit.

Rachel's eyes went from the roll, half illuminated

by the candle, to Kelvin. "So when the Northern Hemisphere is tilted toward the sun, that's summer for us."

Kelvin nodded. "Right."

"And winter for Australia and the rest of the Southern Hemisphere?"

"Right again! For one, being tilted toward the sun means days are longer." Kelvin began to twist the ends of the toothpick between his fingers, making the roll spin. Each point on the roll's surface rotated in and out of the light, sort of like the earth in a day. But the upper side of the roll, which was tilted toward the candle to represent Northern Hemisphere summer, stayed in the light longer. "This is why summer has such long, lovely days. The closer you get to the poles, the bigger this effect gets. Look closely. You can see that the very top of the roll, where the toothpick comes out, doesn't get dark as long as it's tilted toward the candle. That's the North Pole. If you and your parents took a trip to the North Pole right now, you might have trouble sleeping, because the sun stays up all day. It won't get dark there for another three months."

Rachel's eyes grew wide. Henry had heard all of this before, but seeing the roll in the candlelight helped him really understand it. He wondered whether, someday, he would travel to the North Pole himself. During summer, of course. Otherwise he might end up with the opposite problem, which is twenty-four-hour darkness.

"Summer is also hot, because being tilted toward the sun means that sunlight comes down straighter," Kelvin continued. "This allows more light to make it through the atmosphere and, more importantly, the light doesn't get spread out as much when it hits the ground."

Vanessa leaned forward. "Like the difference between noon and evening, right? The sun warms things up a lot more at noon, when it's overhead."

Kelvin nodded happily, his dinner forgotten. "Exactly correct. So it's the tilt of the Earth that determines seasons. All of the things that make the summer warm when our hemisphere is tilted toward the Sun become less present as the earth revolves and we get tilted away from it. Summer,

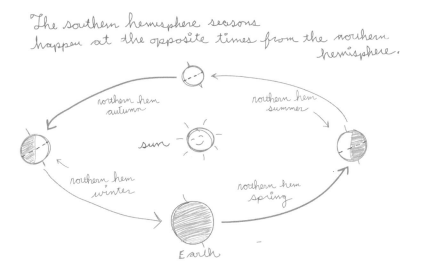

The southern hemisphere seasons happen at the opposite times from the northern hemisphere.

northern hem autumn

northern hem summer

sun

northern hem winter

northern hem spring

Earth

fall, winter, and spring. That's the seasonal cycle. And since the North and South Poles can't both be tilted toward the sun at the same time, the seasons are always opposite in the Northern and Southern Hemispheres. When it's summer here, it's winter there. This doesn't matter as much near the equator, though. Those places are relatively warm all year. They don't have the same sort of seasons we do."

Clarence set a rib bone down on his plate and reclined back, wiping the corner of his mouth with a napkin. "I heard we get seasons—hiccup—'cause the earth gets closer and farther from the sun. That's not true?"

Kelvin shook his head. "It's true that the earth's orbit isn't a perfect circle, but rather an ellipse, so it does get a little closer and farther from the sun as it goes around. That affects things a little bit, but it's not the main cause of the seasons. If it was, the whole planet would have the same seasons at the same time."

"Plus," Henry said, "Earth is closest to the sun in January, which is winter for us."

"Well that is interesting," slurred Clarence, taking a drink.

Kelvin looked back to his neglected meal. He got as far as peppering his broccoli before he spoke up again.

"Oh, and there's one more thing. The tilt of

the earth also influences the direction of sunrise and sunset. For us, in summer, the sun rises and sets a bit farther to the north. In winter, it rises and sets a bit farther south. If you're trying to navigate somewhere without a compass, this can be important to know. This morning, for instance, the sun rose about thirty degrees to the north of due east. So it didn't rise exactly in the east, but a bit north of that."

Vanessa nodded, checking her lipstick. Clarence's eyelids fluttered. But across the table from Henry, Rachel reached out and took the roll from Kelvin. She rotated it around the candle, her freckles blazing in the light. Henry, mouth half full of green beans, couldn't help grinning.

The conversation soon turned to other things and, between jokes and bursts of laughter, they all finished their dinners. Rachel laughed along with her father's boorish jokes and Vanessa started a dialogue with Kelvin about the state of foreign politics, which Henry tried to follow without much success. Through all of this happy commotion, that feeling of warmth and safety from before stayed with Henry. Despite everything, he realized he was glad to be here with Kelvin, through thick and thin.

The check soon came. Before Clarence could say a word, Kelvin pronounced that dinner was his treat and snatched the check away.

Kelvin's phone rang. Rummaging through his cat-painted overcoat, he took a few steps away from the dinner table to answer it.

Rachel tapped Henry's hand. "Storm's still banging on."

Henry looked up, becoming aware of the gusty patter of rain on the roof again. It sounded much nicer from indoors. When they headed back outside, he'd be ready for it.

Henry glanced to his uncle. A pause lingered in Kelvin's conversation, one that was hard to miss. Kelvin's features had taken on a grim appearance.

"I see..." Kelvin said the words with an uncomfortable seriousness. "When did it start?"

The Willowbys noticed as well. The table became quiet.

Another long pause. "Well, thank you for telling me. We'll be right over. Goodbye."

Kelvin shut his phone and turned back to the table. Henry, Rachel, Vanessa, and Clarence all stared at him.

Kelvin wore a grave expression on his face.

"That was Frank Rosenbloom," he said after some hesitation. "Mr. Wrightly's mansion is burning to the ground."

Chapter Eighteen

A Fire for the Dead

Cramming into the car, the party of five sped down the wet roads of Sandy Run. Dusk had passed while they ate, and now the rain fell in torrents from a black sky. Kelvin offered to drop the Willowbys off at the hotel, but they refused, an intense fascination visible on each of their faces. A morbid curiosity about the fire stung at Henry as well. Thunder rattled the windows of the cramped, humid automobile as they hurtled onward.

Henry leaned forward, staring past Clarence's broad shoulder through the rain-soaked windshield. Even from a distance, he could tell that something terrible was happening ahead. Out there, through the darkness and swirling rain, he saw the slight rise of Edward Wrightly's massive estate.

But at the top, where the house should have been, there blazed an awful, offensive brightness.

As they sped closer, Henry could make out

more details. A tall fire twisted around the great mansion in huge columns, reaching toward the sky. It belched out a tower of black smoke, which billowed and swirled into the storm above.

Kelvin skidded the car to a halt. All five people tumbled out into the rain. An assortment of fire trucks lined the front of the house, occupying the driveway and part of the yard, their lights spinning hectically and their crews spraying jets of water up onto the blaze.

Off to the side and farther from the house, a collection of people watched from under raincoats and umbrellas as that yellow-white inferno consumed the manor. Grabbing their raingear, Henry and the others headed up the muddy yard toward the crowd. Frank and Josephina Rosenbloom stood near the back.

"Mr. Rosenbloom," Henry called out. "What happened?"

Frank didn't answer. He stared at the fire. Even from two hundred feet away, Henry felt the heat radiating off it. Sharp cracks and pops sizzled out from the blaze. Henry tried again, shouting this time.

"Mr. Rosenbloom!"

Startled, Frank turned.

"Oh, it's you, Henry," he shouted back. "Terrible, isn't it?" His eyes shifted up to Kelvin.

"How did this start?" Kelvin asked.

Beside her husband, tall, graceful Josephina Rosenbloom turned her eyes to them. "The lightning, we're told."

In the distance, peals of thunder added to the cacophony of the fire.

"No way this was lightning," Henry shouted to Rachel. His thoughts shot back to Mr. Pen, the unpleasant owner of the Sandy Run Inn. That man hated Ed Wrightly. The will dictated that this place would become a bed and breakfast, and now it was burning down. Mr. Pen had every reason to want to avoid competition.

"Yeah," Rachel agreed. "Someone did this."

Josephina heard the statement. Her lips parted. "Someone? You—you don't think all these awful things are happening on purpose, do you, Mr. McCloud?"

"Yes, I do."

Frank and Josephina looked at each other, Josephina biting her lip. Clarence Willowby clutched Vanessa's hand. Somewhere far behind the house, a bolt of lightning jolted downward over the ocean.

Henry looked around. The glow of the inferno illuminated the faces of the other people on the lawn. Nearby, Eugene and Isabel Cook huddled together under a single large golf umbrella. Beside them, Elena Salmon stood with Rodger, saying nothing but holding his pockmarked hand. A little farther away, Victoria Sharp stood beside a geeky-looking man. Walter Sharp, Henry thought. To Victoria's other side, arms crossed, stood a teenage boy with messy blond hair.

Henry recognized him at once. There, not twenty feet away, stood the teenager from Edward Wrightly's mansion. Henry turned toward them, but Kelvin grabbed his shoulder. "Wait. Let's go together."

Together, they strode across the wet lawn.

"Mrs. Sharp," Kelvin said loudly.

Victoria Sharp turned. She gasped. In an instant, all of her composure from the bank was gone. The teenager, seeing Henry and Kelvin in the same instant, took a step back, eyes wide.

"Go," Victoria hissed. "Run." She tried to give him a shove, but slipped on the wet grass and crumpled to the ground. The boy took a few faltering steps away, then sprinted down the wet lawn.

Neither Henry nor Kelvin pursued the boy. "Mrs. Sharp," Kelvin repeated sternly. He offered his hand, but Victoria pushed it away. She rose slowly on her own, her right side now covered with grass and mud. Behind her small round spectacles, her eyes burned with cold intensity.

"You two are such pains," she hissed, "you know that? I answered your questions at the bank. Can't you just leave us alone?"

Henry shook his head. Rachel arrived beside

him. "He's your son, I presume," said Kelvin.

Victoria stamped her foot, glaring fiercely, her disheveled red hair looking like fire in the light of the flames. "No, of course not. I've never met him. Perhaps you can stop sticking that awful nose of yours where it doesn't belong!"

Walter Sharp turned to Victoria, noticing belatedly that something had happened. "What's wrong, Victoria? What's going on?" She slapped his hands away.

Henry stared at the furious woman. He'd come to the same conclusion as his uncle. He remembered that distinctive porcelain bird in Ed Wrightly's study. It looked as if it had lost its companion. The other one, he now remembered, was in Victoria's office. A gift from her thieving son.

The picture frame missing from Victoria's desk was another clue. That's where people usually kept family photos. She had hidden it because she knew they would recognize her son.

Victoria smoldered at them. In the next instant, her eyes shifted. "No," she mouthed. Henry turned and saw, through the billows of rain, the long-haired teenager trudging back across the lawn. He stopped five feet from them, breathing heavy, his long hair dripping with rain. He shook slightly, hands deep in his pockets.

"I, uh, you're that detective, right?" he said, his voice trembling.

"Yes, I am."

The teen looked away, momentarily pressing his eyes shut. "Well, uh, I decided this would be best. I... I want to confess. I've been stealing a little from that place." He motioned up the hill, to the burning mansion.

A drawn-out "What?" came from Walter Sharp.

Kelvin ignored the remark. "Go on."

The teen's breaths were quick and shallow. He rubbed his foot on the muddy ground. "Well, I know you saw me yesterday, when I ran. And, like, I knew it wouldn't be long till you found me. But with what's happening now, I thought maybe I should just confess. Take the punishment. I... I just wanted a motorbike, that's all, and I figured the old guy wouldn't need his stuff anymore. But with the fire and everything, I don't want to be blamed for anything else. I could have been in there, you know."

Kelvin stared at the boy. "What's your name?"

The teen looked at his parents. Victoria glowered at him. "Kyle," he said.

"And did you have anything to do with the fire, Kyle?"

"Now wait just a minute!" Walter interjected, taking a step forward. "Of course my boy didn't have anything to do with this. It was the lightning, didn't you hear?"

Kelvin gritted his teeth. "Excuse me, sir, but I'd

prefer to hear Kyle's account from him. So I repeat. Did you have anything to do with the fire?"

"No, no way," Kyle stammered. Victoria strode to his other side, glaring at Kelvin over dripping glasses.

"And the murder?" Kelvin asked.

"Mu- murder?"

"Mr. Wrightly's death," Henry clarified.

"Don't be absurd!" Victoria screeched. "He would never. He's just a child."

Kelvin fixed her with a look, then returned his attention to Kyle. "Did you have anything to do with the death?"

"No way. Oh man, you mean he got murdered?"

Kelvin nodded. "Would you mind telling me where you were at nine fifteen that night?"

"Uh, at home, with Dad."

Kelvin turned to Walter Sharp. "Is this true?"

"Yes, that's correct," Walter replied.

Rachel put her hands on her hips. She studied Kyle up and down. "So what about the kids with you on the other nights, huh? Who were they?"

Kyle still shook. Walter held the umbrella over him, patting his back, but Kyle continued to drip with rain. "Just friends."

Victoria clenched her teeth. "See, Mr. McCloud, it was all just kids' stuff. No need to harass my family about it."

Kelvin's gray eyes stared at Victoria over his

long nose. "Larceny is a serious crime, Mrs. Sharp, as is receiving stolen goods. I don't need to remind you of that."

Henry stared up at Edward Wrightly's burning home. "The weird thing is, they probably saved whatever they stole."

Kelvin nodded, staring at the Sharps. "Now listen carefully, all three of you, because I'm only going to make this offer once. Make sure it goes to charity. Every last bit of it. Make certain. If that happens we'll overlook this. I didn't come down here to look into burglaries, but I can make an exception if you don't comply. Understand?"

Walter Sharp didn't reply. Victoria nodded. "Yes," she said through gritted teeth. "Of course. Every bit of it. I promise."

Henry turned away. He had heard enough. That teenager, Kyle, had been one of their last leads about the murder. Now that was gone, too. Rachel walked with him. Soon they stood side by side, watching the hideous glare of the fire. Rain continued to pour down, but neither that nor the firemen seemed to have any effect on the tower of flame.

Behind Henry, Clarence Willowby spoke up, having to shout. "Think the murderer did this, guys?"

"Probably," Rachel said.

"But why? Why now?"

Rachel and Henry turned to Clarence in unison. "What?"

"I don't understand," he explained, still wobbling slightly. "Why burn down a dead guy's house? What's there to gain?"

Kelvin had returned, looking frustrated, but he didn't have an answer for this question either. Henry's mind went to Mr. Pen again, but even there, something didn't feel quite right. He felt as if he was forgetting something. But who else was there? The Cooks? The Rosenblooms? All had solid alibis.

Henry looked at his uncle. "Learn anything else from Victoria?"

Dripping with rain, Kelvin shook his head.

"Ask about that light in her house?" Rachel asked. "The one Frank Rosenbloom saw at two a.m.?"

"I did, but I had guessed the answer already. When Victoria heard the teenagers at Wrightly's manor that night, she suspected her son was up there. She went into his bedroom and turned on the light. She found the room empty. Simple as that."

Henry rubbed his wet hair. "Great. That doesn't help us one bit."

At the far end of the yard, a sudden loud, shuddering creak rang out, and the manor sagged. The sound of snapping timber crackled from within and, slowly, the huge house's left half started to collapse. Cinders flew into the sky as the once great manor crumpled in on itself.

A pang of sadness cut into Henry. He had been so amazed by the place when they first saw it, days ago. It had been filled with untold stories and mysteries, a life filled with complexity and failures and success.

And now here it stood, meeting its end.

Like its owner.

Henry stood beside Rachel, watching in silence as the house collapsed. "It's been a long day," Vanessa said wearily. "Maybe we should get home."

Chapter Nineteen

Mr. Wrightly's Shadow

Five a.m., in darkness. That's when Kelvin shook Henry awake. Dragging himself from bed, Henry changed into shorts and a T-shirt and followed Kelvin to the lobby. He wanted to ask Mr. Pen a few questions, but the girl at the front desk looked at Henry with bleary eyes.

"He's probably in bed," she told him. "Like we all should be."

Henry agreed. Even the stiff hotel bed sounded nice right now. He closed his eyes, but the jostling, bumping car ride kept him from falling back into his dreams of swirling infernos, black and white towers reaching into the blue sky, and a girl with a ponytail sitting on popcorn clouds. Over the churn of the engine, he heard his uncle talking.

"Sorry about the hour, Henry, but returning to Wrightly's manor before dawn is crucial. We need to investigate before the police arrive."

Henry kept his eyes shut and nodded. He thought about Rachel. She was still in bed, no doubt. After their late night, Kelvin had told her to sleep in. But there would be no sleeping in for Henry, not today.

The car bumped to a stop. Henry opened his eyes. They sat halfway up the dead man's driveway. The sun hadn't risen yet, so a dark stillness hung over the yard. The only light came from the faint gray illumination to the east, out over the ocean. It silhouetted the collapsed remains of the house, making everything a little eerie.

Henry got out. The stink of ash lingered in the salt air. The crunch of stones beneath their feet and the distant lapping of ocean waves did little to disrupt the stagnant silence surrounding the remains of the manor. In the center of the heap of rubble, only a great central spire of timbers and bricks remained upright. It looked like a tombstone, topped with an ornate rooster weathervane. That weathervane used to tell the direction of the wind, but now it stood seared and broken.

Kelvin and Henry crossed into the yard, stopping at the edge of the debris. Henry pushed through a few pieces with his foot, moving aside burnt, broken timbers, scorched bricks, and shattered glass, all covered by a layer of warm gray ash. The stink, unable to leave in the stillness of the morning air, was overwhelming up close.

Kelvin didn't seem to mind. He squatted down and picked up a plank, examining it with his eyes and fingers. Without putting it to his nose, he handed it to Henry.

Henry smelled it. Despite the stink of ash, he could detect something else, something that even the rain hadn't been able to eradicate from the deep cracks. "Gasoline. Definitely."

Kelvin nodded in satisfied silence, then looked at other pieces of rubble. Walking the other way, Henry kicked aside pieces of ruined house. Under bricks and wood and ash lay some of Mr. Wrightly's personal belongings, things collected over a lifetime of travel. None had survived the fire.

In the mass of rubble ahead, Henry spotted the sharp angles of Mr. Wrightly's large black sedan, but it no longer provoked the cold shiver down Henry's spine that it once had. The automobile lay crushed and seared under the fallen car shelter.

Rachel should be here. That's what Henry wanted. She would have some new way of looking at things. Even if she didn't, she would make this place feel less like an awful, collapsed mausoleum.

Henry returned to his uncle. "Find anything?"

Kelvin circled his way around the wreckage, inspecting the remains. "No."

"Are we sure the murderer did this?"

Kelvin leaned over, picked up a burnt shingle, and then tossed it aside. "Almost certainly. But the question remains. With Wrightly already dead, why bother?"

"To get rid of evidence? We found the letters inside, after all."

Kelvin nodded distractedly. Henry's mind lingered on Mr. Pen, but he said nothing about that. What was he forgetting?

Henry and Kelvin continued around the wreckage. As light slowly crept across the sky, the estate became easier to see, but it didn't help. Nothing useful remained. Everything was burnt and destroyed.

At the far side of the wreckage, Kelvin sat down. In the flattened grass beside him, Henry sat too. The pale light over the ocean gradually spread and became yellower. As the world slowly turned to allow them a view of the sun, at least they would have good seats.

"The light will help," Henry said.

Kelvin nodded. He leaned back on his hands and looked out at the ocean with tired eyes.

A sliver of sun started to peek over the horizon, its rays illuminating the water's surface and glittering off moving waves. The few thin clouds became whiter, and seagulls on the beach squawked and stretched their wings. Henry didn't like getting up so early, but moments like this were worth it. There was something tranquil about sunrises. They lacked the fierce red of sunsets. Henry and Kelvin's long shadows stretched back over the grass toward the remains of the house.

Kelvin reached out a hand and patted Henry on the shoulder. "I want you to know something, Henry. I'm glad you came. Even if we can't solve the murder, I'm glad you're here."

Henry felt a calm warmth rise up in him, like the feeling from the restaurant last night, only stronger. As Kelvin said, even if they couldn't find the murderer, just being here, watching this sunrise together, was enough. A thorough sense of peace ran through Henry, the sort of feeling he hadn't experienced since his parents disappeared.

He and Kelvin really did sail in the same boat, after all. Henry sometimes forgot, but when he lost his parents on that awful day eight months ago, Kelvin lost a sister.

Henry took a deep breath. He had something to say. He rubbed his hands together awkwardly.

"I'm sorry, you know, for yelling at you the other day. I was just upset. I didn't mean it."

Kelvin smiled. "I know. You were right, though. I'm not your father, and I can't replace him." He wrapped an arm around Henry's shoulder. "But I'm going to do the best I can for you anyway."

And with that, with a few simple words, everything felt right once more. Even if his parents weren't there, Henry finally had a family again.

Henry turned where he sat and gave his uncle

a fierce hug.

Elbows on knees, the two sat for several minutes more, watching the sun rise over the ocean and hearing the sea wash against sand on the beach. Kelvin stood. He held out his hand.

"Come on. What do you say we finish this case?"

Henry nodded resolutely. Grabbing his uncle's hand, he rose to his feet.

Henry and Kelvin circled the ruined manor one last time, searching for clues. Nothing new lay on the ground, but Henry noticed the rooster weather-vane again. It topped the last remaining spire in the center of the rubble, now brightly illuminated in the sun. The cast iron rooster seemed to crow the arrival of a new day. Henry continued to walk. The lone spire cast a great, long shadow, which stretched out over the rubble and across the front yard.

Henry's heart jolted. He almost missed a step. He stared at that shadow. That colossally, magnificently, monumentally important shadow. The gears and levers in his brain began to grind and move.

Astonished, Henry turned to his uncle. Kelvin stared at the spire's shadow too. A look of surprise leapt onto his face. "Henry!" he said.

Henry didn't need to be told. In a flash, they bounded to the front yard and stood side by side, their backs to the ruined house and the magnificent sun, staring across the lawn.

In this moment, all of the clues started coming together. The uncertainty that had hung over Henry like a fog began to burn away in the morning sun.

Kelvin smacked himself on the forehead. "Of course! Why didn't I see it sooner?"

With a look of immense satisfaction on his face, he turned to Henry and said the words he had clearly wanted to say for days.

"I know exactly who murdered Edward Wrightly."

Chapter Twenty

What the Clues Reveal

Henry could have laughed, had their surroundings seemed less deathly serious. Some details still eluded him, but the main points of the solution were becoming clearer and clearer. The shadow of Ed Wrightly's single remaining spire proved to be all he and Kelvin needed for the pieces to fall into place.

Kelvin took a few resolute steps through the flattened grass, heading down the lawn, but faltered and stopped. A look of indecision came onto his face. He turned toward Henry. "Well, did you figure it out?"

"I think so."

"Good. Let's work through it from the beginning, just to be sure. If we're going to accuse someone of murder, we can't have missed something important."

Kelvin was right. A good theory couldn't have

big holes. Henry pictured his father again, and Arthur Alabaster's words rang in his head.

Whenever you can, Henry, think through an idea yourself. This is vitally important. Ask others, definitely, but always remember to think. You'll be a better person for it.

"Okay," Henry said, thinking back to the beginning. "I'll go through what we know. First, the light behind Ed Wrightly's house, the original fire, was seen at nine fifteen p.m., six days ago."

"Yes, that's where things began. Go on."

Henry went on deliberately, weighing the details. "Considering how things turned out, I think we can say someone was trying to burn the manor down that night. We know the lightning didn't make that black mark, and the umbrella scrap suggests that someone else was in the yard with the dead man. The person probably picked that night because a fire would be blamed on the storm." Henry paused. It was difficult to keep all the facts straight, but he spoke carefully. "That brings us to point number two: Ed Wrightly liked working late."

"True," Kelvin agreed again, playing Watson for a change. Henry would be Sherlock this time. "We learned that fact from Victoria Sharp. He obsessed over his work and rarely left before midnight."

"But on that night," Henry said, "he left work at nine. Frank Rosenbloom saw a car pull up the driveway at nine fifteen, just after seeing the light from the fire. That's much sooner than Ed usually got home."

"Okay, so what of it?"

Kelvin was testing him, Henry knew. He paused, checking his logic, before going on. "Well, whoever was trying to burn down the house that night probably didn't expect Ed home so early. On most nights, he wouldn't have gotten back for hours. That makes me think the person just wanted to burn down the house, not murder Ed Wrightly."

Kelvin gave a small exclamation. "Good! That's what gave me difficulty for the longest time. I kept asking myself, 'Who wanted to kill Wrightly?' when I should have been asking, 'Who wanted to destroy his home?'" He stopped, clearing his throat. "Go on."

Henry grinned. His skin tingled. "Okay, so we found the burn mark at the back corner of the house, near where the car shelter is. The sound and light from a car coming up the driveway would usually have been pretty noticeable, but perhaps not in a storm like that. I think the arsonist got caught off guard. When Ed Wrightly pulled his car in, they both saw each other. Ed probably made a run for it. That's when he got murdered: on his way to his front door. He wasn't running from the hail, but from a person."

Kelvin nodded solemnly. "And the murder weapon?"

Henry paused. All he could think of was Rodger

208

Salmon's baseball bat, but that wasn't right.

"Remember the dead man's missing umbrella?" Kelvin said. "Frank Rosenbloom told us about it. Why do you think it went missing? I imagine the murderer was trying to get rid of evidence. Frank told us that the umbrella had a heavy steel handle, dented noticeably. It could have made a convenient weapon in a pinch. Once the arsonist started to panic, I don't think an older man like Wrightly had much of a chance."

Henry imagined that night again. He saw the arsonist wrestling with Ed Wrightly in the dark, with hailstones streaking down around them and thunder crashing in the distance. And then, crack. A sour sickness churned in Henry's stomach.

"So the hail…" he started.

"Was probably just good luck for the murderer. The bruises Wrightly received while he lay dying in the storm did a good job obscuring the fatal blow."

The sick feeling in Henry's stomach didn't go away. It was such an awful, stupid thing to happen to anyone.

Henry shook his head, trying to clear away the gruesome details. He returned to his original point. "But all of this happened because someone wanted to get rid of Ed's house."

"So who wanted to do that?"

"A lot of people." Henry's mind immediately

went to Mr. Pen, the obnoxious owner of the Sandy Run Inn. "Mr. Pen, for one. This place was supposed to become a bed and breakfast after Ed died. We learned that from the will. Mr. Pen wouldn't have liked competing with a new place. He's had money troubles in the past, and maybe he didn't want to risk losing his hotel. He definitely hated Ed Wrightly. He told us that himself. But..." Here, Henry finally remembered the detail he had been missing. "He also told us he hated fire! No way he would do this. Besides, even if he did know the will, he wouldn't need to burn the house while Ed was still alive. Plus, Frank Rosenbloom only saw one car go up the driveway that night, so I think it was someone in the neighborhood."

"Good. Very thorough. So Mr. Pen didn't do it. Who else might have motive? Process of elimination. Let's make sure it couldn't have been any of our other suspects."

Henry glanced around himself. If the murderer was who he suspected, it might be unwise to discuss this for too long. Still, no cars were in the driveways across the street, so they were probably safe.

"It could have been Victoria Sharp's son, Kyle," Henry said. "I know Walter Sharp assured us the kid was at home on the night of the murder, but we can't be sure he told us the truth. Kyle could have been stealing from Ed's house for weeks and wanted to get rid of the place to destroy the evidence. But the notes from the study tell us someone tried to get him to move away last year, so that doesn't really work. Victoria herself might have wanted the house gone. She probably hated living next to her boss and could have sent the notes to scare him away. When he didn't leave, she could've gotten more desperate. But we know where she and Rodger Salmon were that night."

"Maybe they snuck out her office window," Kelvin suggested, "and came back afterward. Rodger did have all those hailstone bruises, you know."

Henry considered the idea for a minute, but shook his head. "No. That big window in Victoria's office doesn't open. I noticed that when we visited her. No latch. Rodger must have gotten those bruises when he left. The storm was still going on, I think."

Kelvin smiled slyly. "Good. So let's review what we know. Don't forget when those threatening letters were sent. Last summer and just recently."

"Yeah. We know that someone wanted the house gone, and we know from the letters that it made them especially angry in summer."

"Anything else?"

Henry's mind pitched forward in top gear now, working furiously. "We know that the hail was strong enough to bruise people, like what happened to Rodger Salmon and Ed Wrightly. Since the murderer got his umbrella torn up, he should have those bruises too."

"So who, other than Rodger and the dead man, has bruises?"

Henry stopped and thought. "No one." How could that be? The thought only delayed him a second. "But bruises can be covered up. With makeup... or with long clothes!"

"I didn't see anyone caked with makeup," Kelvin said. "And who would wear long clothes in summer?"

A smile came to Henry's face. "Not many people. But we did meet two. They live in the same house." And here, Henry looked away from his uncle. He and Kelvin both stood in the shade of that last remaining spire, and their eyes followed the spire's long shadow across the front yard. It streamed across the lawn, passed over the road, and ended directly on top of one of the distant houses on the far side. One house in particular.

Henry said the names softly, lest, even from this great distance, they somehow hear. "Eugene and Isabel Cook."

Henry paused, letting the names hang in the air. He pictured Eugene's paint-covered seersuckers and Isabel's long blue-green bathrobe. Either of them could hide the painful bruises.

"Hmm..." Kelvin said. "Scandalous. So they both did it?"

"No. I don't think so. Being out in bad weather

can cause you to get sick more easily, like Isabel was, but plenty of people saw her at the book club. She stayed there all night."

Henry took a deep breath, and then continued. "No, the murderer was Eugene."

Kelvin remained silent for a handful of seconds, staring across the lawn at the Cook's tan, two-story house. They were long, solemn seconds. "Yes," Kelvin said, "the murderer should have hailstone bruises, and yes, they can be hidden under long clothes. Long clothes aren't proof of murder, though. We need to be sure, Henry. Eugene said he was at the movies that night."

Henry nodded, now certain of his theory. "Eugene claims he was at the movies. Afterward he said he stood next to his car and watched the storm, waiting for it to let up. But he lied. We saw his car. It was all dented up from the hail. There's no way he stood next to it that night."

Kelvin shrugged. "So what? He got confused. What about the movie ticket he had?"

"He could have gotten that any time. Doesn't mean he stayed for the movie."

"And the power outage? He knew when the theater lost power. I checked, remember, and he was right."

"He could have called and asked the next day." But Henry was growing tired of answering his uncle's questions, so he laid out his theory. "Here's what I think. Isabel saw Eugene head to the movies that night, and Eugene took steps to pretend he stayed there, but he went back home instead. That's how his car got all dented up. With his wife at the book club and a storm whipping about outside, nobody noticed when he got back. He'd sent letters to try to get Ed Wrightly to move away, so he could burn down an empty house, but it hadn't worked. Edward wouldn't move.

"So Eugene took his umbrella and some gasoline and went to burn the house down anyway, thinking Ed would work late like normal. He must have panicked when Ed got home. Maybe he didn't mean to, but he murdered Ed Wrightly then and there. In a panic, he pushed the ivy lattice in front of the burn mark and ran, and then retrieved Ed Wrightly's umbrella the next day. He waited for another storm before he went back to finish the job.

"If he has those hailstone bruises, we'll know it was him. I know none of our evidence is perfect, but I think together it will be enough. He'll have to make up a new alibi for last night, too. He's finished."

Henry looked at his uncle. After a moment, Kelvin nodded. "I think you're right. It's a solid theory. But you've left something out. The motive. Why did Eugene do it?"

Henry's mouth fell open. He couldn't believe it. How'd he forget the biggest piece of the puzzle? That's what had made everything click into place.

Before answering, Henry turned 180 degrees and looked exactly away from the Cooks' tan, two-story house. In front of him lay the ruined manor and, on the far side, the Atlantic Ocean. The soft yellows of the morning stretched out across the sky above. But directly in front of Henry, exactly where the sun should have been, stood the last remaining pillar of the massive manor, an imposing black mass against the lovely pastel sky, blocking the view.

"Eugene did it," Henry explained, "because of the sunrise. Ed Wrightly's huge manor got in the way."

Kelvin nodded again, a grim expression on his face. "And not even for the whole year. Just the summer. Since sunrises move throughout the year, the house only really got in the way during the summer."

Henry had pieced most of his theory together minutes ago, but only now, once the words came out, did everything really start to sink in. All of this awfulness, all of this pain, because of a sunrise? A foul, indignant anger boiled up in Henry's chest. He could hardly believe his own theory.

"Ed Wrightly is dead because his house got in the way of a sunrise," Henry said. "That's just…"

He didn't go on. He couldn't. The long shadow stretched across the lawn like a bony finger from beyond the grave, pointing out the murderer. It all made sense, after all—the threatening notes, sent only in the summer; the lovingly painted sunrises in Eugene's guest room; Victoria's claim that Eugene always got ornery when he missed one. When all of the pieces of the puzzle had been fitted together, this was the picture it made.

Henry hated it. Hated, hated, hated it. But he couldn't deny it. He had learned long ago that when you are presented with a conclusion, and all of the evidence points to it being true, you aren't allowed to toss it aside simply because you don't like it.

Henry looked up. Kelvin was watching him. He had a soft, sad look in his eyes. "What you're thinking is right, Henry. It was an awful thing for Eugene to do, and petty. But sometimes people are awful and petty. Not most people, and not most of the time, but if someone never learns the right way to treat others, it can happen.

"Eugene probably hated that the manor blocked his view. He might also have believed that getting rid of it would help his chances of renting out his house. You remember what he said, don't you? 'It will have a wonderful view.' Maybe he didn't really mean to kill Wrightly that night. Maybe it was an accident." Kelvin paused, and a resolute, furious look came into his eyes. "But that doesn't excuse him."

Henry stared across the lawn at Eugene's house again. Finally, the pieces had fallen into place. At last Henry could fill in that shadowy figure he kept picturing standing over Ed Wrightly on the night of the murder. No longer was it a faceless phantom, but portly, drawling Eugene Cook.

Kelvin took out his phone. "Now that we're sure, I'll call the police." He pressed several keys, but then stopped. He shook the phone. Moisture clouded the inside of the dark screen. "Must have gotten soaked in the storm last night. Poor planning on my part." He snapped the phone shut.

Henry stamped his foot. "Phone or not, we have to make sure Eugene doesn't get away with this."

"Rest assured, he won't. It looks like he might be gone right now, but his wife can probably tell us where he went. We'll find a way to call the police once we know where he is."

Henry nodded firmly. Then, side-by-side, they marched down the hill and crossed the street. Striding across the lawn, they banged on the door.

A sick, tired, vaguely surprised Isabel Cook appeared.

"Is Eugene here?" Henry said.

"Well no, honey," Isabel replied through sniffles. "He's gone to do some errands before work. Left just before sunrise, about fifteen minutes ago."

She paused to sneeze several times.

"I think," she continued, "he was heading for the Sandy Run Inn, to see the two of you."

Chapter Twenty-One

Hailstones

Without a word between them, Henry and Kelvin sprinted from Isabel Cook's door and headed back across the lawn. The car sent gravel flying into the air as Kelvin sped back toward the hotel.

Rachel. That's all Henry could think. He wasn't sure why Eugene would come to see them, or what would happen next, but it couldn't be anything good. That note from yesterday morning, staked to their door, kept flashing in his mind.

Leave. Or else.

And they hadn't left. Eugene knew this. He was at the fire last night. Eugene had met Rachel too, and after failing to find Henry and Kelvin, wouldn't he go to her room next?

Henry didn't want to think about it. Why weren't they there yet? Certainly he would have a full gray beard and missing teeth before they arrived.

Ahead, the entrance of the Sandy Run Inn jumped into sight. Henry caught a glimpse of a dented blue sedan in the parking lot, but he couldn't tell if it was Eugene's. As soon as they stopped, he leapt from the car, Kelvin just behind. They ran through the great glass doors at the hotel entrance, the small brass bell chiming wildly.

Behind the counter, Mr. Pen jumped in his seat, eyes wide at the sudden intrusion. "Now wait just a minute!"

Henry wanted to keep running, but his uncle skidded to a halt.

"A man—" Kelvin started rapidly. "Did a man just go upstairs? Not one of your guests, but a middle-aged southern man?"

"What's this about?" Mr. Pen demanded.

"Just answer!"

Mr. Pen recoiled. He fumbled with papers on his desk. "Well, ah, yes, I suppose. Five minutes ago."

Henry ran to the desk. "And did he come back down?"

Mr. Pen's eyes darted between them. "Well, no... not that I saw, but I was in back a minute ago."

Kelvin turned to the stairs. "Call the police," he said after a moment's pause. "There's a murderer in your hotel. Tell them to come to the third and second floors."

The second floor. Rachel's floor.

"A murderer? In my hotel?"

"Just call."

Henry started for the stairs. Kelvin strode a pace behind. They took the stairs two at a time, darting upward in a rapid, measured run.

At the second floor, Rachel's floor, Henry stopped. His heart pounded. His mouth felt dry. Thoughts flew through his head so fast it was hard to concentrate on them. Kelvin passed him, heading up to the next floor, but the murderer wasn't there, Henry knew. He shook his head. No, he didn't know that. He feared it.

Kelvin glanced back. Henry felt certain now. "We need to check here first," he said.

Indecision lingered in Kelvin's stance. He looked down at Henry from seven or eight steps up. He gave a short, decisive nod.

Bounding back down the steps, Kelvin pushed himself between Henry and the stairwell door. "But I go first." Leaning close, he put his ear to the wood.

Kelvin remained quiet for a beat. Then, stepping back, he pulled the door open. Beyond stretched an empty hallway. No Eugene Cook, no anybody. Rachel's room lay around the next corner, out of sight.

Henry and Kelvin stole out into the hall, Henry letting the door close softly behind them. At the corner, they flattened themselves against the gold-flecked wallpaper. Henry's heart thumped so loudly he feared it would give them away. Kelvin put a finger to his lips and they listened. Two faint voices came from somewhere out of sight.

"No ma'am, it sure isn't that important. If you happen to see him, though, do give me a ring."

An unclear response came from farther away.

"This here's my number. Thank you kindly."

A door shut. Silence persisted for several seconds. Kelvin leaned toward Henry. "I can't let him leave before the police arrive, Henry," he whispered urgently. "We might lose him for good. You go back downstairs." Henry stood his ground. He wasn't leaving with a murderer on Rachel's floor. Come to think of it, he wasn't leaving Kelvin to face this alone. He shook his head fiercely. Soft footsteps approached around the corner.

Despite his determination, the sound cut into Henry, making his head swirl. Kelvin didn't carry a weapon, he knew. "Okay," Kelvin mouthed. "Act normal. Follow my lead."

Henry fought down an urge to panic. He nodded, putting on his most casual face. He and Kelvin stepped away from the corner, away from the safety of concealment, and into the hallway beyond.

Nearly straight into Eugene Cook.

Eugene gave a startled squeal.

"Oh!" said Kelvin.

Henry did his best to act surprised.

Eugene stumbled half a step back. "Well shoot! Mr. McCloud!"

"Mr. Cook!" Kelvin replied. Everybody stood still. "Fancy meeting you here."

Eugene let out what amounted to a nervous laugh. "Well, actually, this is great. Just the man I was searchin' for."

Kelvin raised his eyebrows. "Oh?"

"Sure enough," Eugene croaked. He cleared his throat, then stretched him lips into a smile.

Henry had to concentrate hard not to shiver. Eugene seemed pleasant and earnest and, even now, Henry wished he could believe Eugene was innocent. But, as it was, Eugene's smile only served to cast a stark light onto his horrible deeds.

"Well, it's about last night," Eugene said. "You asked Isabel and me if we saw anything, and darn it, I think I was being unhelpful. As it happens, I remember something."

"Oh?" Kelvin sounded thoroughly interested. It

was a good act. "What was it?"

Eugene rubbed a hand down the back of his neck. He wasn't wearing the paint-smeared seersuckers today, but still wore long clothes that covered all the way from his neck to his hands and down to his shoes. "Well, it's a pinch hard to admit. Truth is I didn't want to say anything at first but, well... I think one of my neighbors had a hand settin' that fire."

Henry felt he should say something. "Really?"

He tried to sound interested, like Kelvin, but the sudden shift of Eugene's eyes told him he had done a bad job. Despite some plumpness around the gut, Eugene remained an imposing man. He stood about a foot taller than Henry, and looked quite a bit stronger. Henry shrank under Eugene's gaze, immediately aware of his jumpy muscles and flushed face.

A pause preceded Eugene's response—just a second or so, but undeniably there. "Why yes, young sir. It's a touchy subject for me, them being our friends and all, but I can't hide the fact any longer. It's about Elena and Rodger Salmon, like you suspected before. I remember a few weeks ago they were saying how much they hated Ed's house. Made a heap of comments like that over the years."

Kelvin rubbed his chin and nodded, not one crack showing in his bluff. "Hmm... Yes, that's very suspicious."

"See, that's precisely what I was thinking," Eugene said. He wrung his hands. "But the worst bit was what I saw last night, after you'd left. When I was headin' home, I saw Rodger. Blow me down, but he was laughing! Just cacklin' away. He tried to hide it when he saw me, but in his hand was a gas can!"

Eugene stopped, his eyes jumping between Kelvin and Henry. He licked his dry lips.

In the silence, Henry heard a faint noise outside the hotel. He could have pumped his fist with joy. From far away came the soft, shrill whine of sirens.

"Well that is something," Kelvin said, still playing along. "I suspected him myself. You know, with that baseball bat and everything."

"I know! Couldn't believe my eyes. Rodger's a good friend of mine."

The sound outside was becoming louder.

"I never figured that—"

Eugene paused. His mouth stayed open, but his eyes had grown wide.

"I never figured..."

The sentence trailed off. The whine of sirens was unmistakable now. Eugene's eyes darted between Kelvin and Henry.

"But..."

The sentence died in his throat. A brief, pleading look came into his eyes.

Kelvin took a step forward, raising his hand. "The game's up, Mr. Cook," he said firmly. "We know it was you. You should just come along quietly."

Eugene took a shaking, hesitant step backward, looking poised to run, but he stumbled to the side and pressed his back to the wall. His mouth opened and shut, but no words came out. His eyes stayed fixed on Kelvin, an awful terror lingering there. But even as he trembled, the look of helplessness fell from his face. His expression contorted with rage and fear.

Eugene reached for something behind his back. In the same instant, he lunged forward.

Henry didn't have time to react. Eugene wrenched him violently to the side and Henry's head struck against the wall. An arm closed around his chest and, before he could even cry out, Eugene Cook stood at his back.

Henry grabbed the arm and kicked back forcefully, struggling to break free, but something stopped him— a cold, sharp touch against his neck. Out of the corner of his eye Henry saw it: a terrible, terrifying thing in Eugene's free hand. It glinted with the bright, cold shine of a knife .

"Now back up!" Eugene shouted in a hoarse,

wavering voice. "Just you back up!"

Kelvin did take a step back, a small one. He held his hands in front of himself. "Now, wait. Calm down, Mr. Cook." The confidence was gone. Kelvin's voice possessed a note Henry had never heard in his uncle before—a sudden, desperate fear.

Eugene took a number of uneven steps backwards, wrenching Henry farther down the hall. Henry felt hot breath on his neck and the rapid, deep movement of Eugene's stomach against his back.

"Just put the knife down," Kelvin said. "It's over. Arson's one thing, but kidnapping is quite another." Arson, kidnapping, but no mention of murder. Henry saw that, even now, Kelvin had his wits.

Eugene's hand trembled. Outside, the sirens wailed. Desperation sounded in Eugene's drawl. "Lord, I don't want to go to jail," he moaned. "Can't we just... Can't you forget it?"

"Let Henry go," Kelvin said. "Then we can talk."

Eugene's breathing quickened; he took short, unsteady steps backwards down the hallway. "You'd just have me arrested. I can see that, plain as day. But you don't understand. It was an accident, I swear. A mistake. I just wanted that house gone. That awful house! But he just looked so terrified, that stupid coward of a man. He just looked so shocked, running like a chicken with its head gone. I—I don't know what came over me. I wanted to make him sorry."

Henry's mind whirled. He needed to do something. Eugene became louder and more deranged with each step. His voice had become a terrified, malicious wail.

"Just let Henry go," Kelvin repeated, following him.

Eugene didn't seem to hear. Outside, the sirens stopped getting louder. Above the window at the end of the hall, pulsating yellow lights shone on the ceiling.

"That vile man!" Eugene yelled. "That vile old man. It's all his fault!"

Kelvin held his hands in front of him, keeping pace with Eugene. "We can talk this through. We can—"

Next to them, a door creaked opened. Bleary-eyed and pajama-clad, Rachel Willowby stepped out.

"Just who's making—" she started. But when she saw Kelvin and Henry and Eugene Cook all standing there, and she saw the knife at Henry's throat, she screamed.

All of Eugene's attention swung to Rachel. He jerked around to face her. Henry felt Eugene's grip suddenly loosen. The knife left his throat. It pointed at Rachel.

At that moment, only one thing came to Henry's

mind.

Hailstones.

All those hailstones pelting down in waves on the night of the murder, lit only by strokes of lightning, like flashes from a camera.

All those ugly hailstone welts on poor Ed Wrightly's body, blotting his skin and disguising the fatal blow.

And, finally, all those sore, painful bruises hidden under the murderer's long clothes.

That was the important bit: those bruises.

Henry wrenched an arm free. He extended it in front of himself. With all his might, he drove his elbow back into Eugene Cook's ribs.

A surprised, painful gasp of air erupted from Eugene's lips. He doubled forward in a spasm. Henry felt Eugene's hold suddenly slip, giving him a chance. Tearing himself free, Henry leapt forward into Rachel.

Together, Henry and Rachel tumbled to the floor in the doorway of her room. Henry looked back just in time to see Kelvin spring forward. The sound of Kelvin's fist meeting Eugene's face cracked down the hallway.

Eugene Cook hit the wall hard. He crumpled to the floor, crying out in agony and surprise. His long knife, spinning through the air, landed several feet away, its shiny blade digging into the carpet.

Eugene clutched his nose in anguish, blood pouring between his fingers.

Around the corner came the sound of police crashing through the stairwell door.

Chapter Twenty-Two

The Woman from New York

The hallway of the Sandy Run Inn soon swam with people.

At first, chaos ensued. Loud, yelling chaos. Not sure who had done what, the police detained everybody. They removed the knife from the scene and made sure that neither Kelvin nor Henry nor Eugene Cook, who was now doubled over on his knees, could move another inch.

But with some help from her parents, Rachel soon set the record straight and Henry and Kelvin were set free.

Rubbing his wrists, Henry staggered away from the crowd. He leaned against the wall. Everything swirled around him. He felt nauseous. Ten feet away, police dragged Eugene Cook to his feet in cuffs.

Eugene looked wild and frightened, his hair in disarray and deep red blood staining his lips and chin. He stammered desperate pleas and struggled against the policemen like a fox in a trap, but it was all for nothing. Henry clutched his chest, trying to slow his breathing.

Squeezing between two policemen, Rachel ran forward. She threw her arms around him.

"Henry, are you all right?" She started looking him over for cuts or bruises. "Are you hurt?"

The hallway whirled, but Henry managed a weak smile. "I'm fine."

Rachel looked him straight in the eye. "I thought you were finished for sure. When I saw him with the knife, and I saw he was holding you, I just..." She didn't finish the sentence. She seemed to be holding back tears. "But what happened? Is he... Is he the murderer?"

Henry nodded. A foul taste lingered in his mouth. "Yeah."

"But why'd he do it? What for?"

Henry slumped down the wall. The spinning in his head slowed, but the frenzied commotion continued around them. "The sunrise," he managed at last. "Ed's house got in the way of the sunrise."

Rachel's mouth hung open. Not one word came out, and Henry could tell that she was thinking exactly the same thing he had.

She closed her mouth tightly. "Well, at least it's over. I don't know what else to say."

"That's enough," Henry said. "At least it's over."

Around them, other people emerged from their rooms, some sleepy-eyed and in pajamas. Mr. Pen pushed his way forward from the back of the crowd, craning his neck and trying to see over people's shoulders. The large businessman and the skinny surfer kid stood pointing and discussing things together.

"Gnarly," the surfer kid said.

"Indeed," replied the businessman. "Gnarly."

Henry rose to his feet again, looking through the throng of people for Kelvin. Kelvin stood on the far side of the crowd, talking to Vanessa and Clarence and the police. He was explaining to them, no doubt, the events that had unfolded over the past few days.

Henry rubbed his head. In the opposite direction, toward the corner that led to the stairwell, the crowd thinned out. But one person caught his attention immediately.

Partially hidden behind a chatting couple stood the woman in the yellow dress - the woman from New York.

The rest of the world dissolved away. Henry stepped forward, trying to get a better look. The woman turned and disappeared around the corner.

Henry brushed past the people in the hallway. That woman wouldn't escape him this time.

Henry thought of his mother. Maybe she hadn't died that day, eight months ago. Maybe she'd come back at last. Where had she been? Was Dad here too? Henry wanted to tell them both just how much he missed them. He wanted to wrap his arms around them and never let go.

Henry rounded the corner. There she was. But she didn't run this time. She simply walked.

"Wait," Henry said.

Ahead, the woman stopped. She seemed to hesitate, her fingers wrapped around the handle of the stairwell door.

Henry stopped too. From here, the murmur of the crowd in the other hallway seemed dim and far away.

So many questions danced on Henry's tongue. So many things needed to be asked and said. Henry wanted see her bright smile and feel the proud clap of Dad's hand against his back. He wanted to go to the mountains with them, and the circus, and spend those cold, rainy days with them, drinking hot cocoa and not doing much of anything at all.

Susan, Arthur, and Henry Alabaster, together again.

But he stopped. It wasn't true. Even before the woman turned around, he knew deep inside that she wasn't his mother.

After a long hesitation, the woman turned to face him. "Yes?"

She seemed timid and jittery, her smooth face pretty but pale. Her blue eyes rested on Henry and she wrung her thin hands.

"Yes?" she repeated. "May I help you?"

Henry didn't recognize the woman at all. That familiar snake in his belly, the one that had been with him these past eight months, constricted suddenly, squeezing the air from his lungs, threatening to suffocate him. He opened his mouth, but no air would come.

No, not his mother. Not even close.

He should have realized from that very first encounter, way back in New York. And perhaps, deep inside, he had. If his parents were still alive, they would have contacted him. A letter. A call. Something. They would have fought against fire and floods to make it back home, just so they could walk through the front door and wrap their arms around him.

A lump rose in Henry's throat. Whatever happened on that plane eight months ago, it didn't really change anything, he realized. It didn't change the fact that they'd been great parents, and it didn't change the fact that he loved them.

Henry smiled. With this, finally, the snake let go. It withered away and fell into dust, and Henry knew that it was gone for good. No more regret over the past. Henry straightened himself. He wiped away tears. He took the cleanest, deepest breath of air he had taken in a long time.

Henry now only had a few questions for the

woman. He started with most obvious.

"Who are you?"

The woman glanced to the stairwell door again, fidgeting with her hands, but she didn't leave. Henry pictured that ornate S. each of the letters had been signed with.

"My name is Silvia Moss," she said at last. "Edward was my neighbor. And you're Henry, right?"

Wiping his nose, Henry nodded. He remembered Rachel's neighborhood map. Silvia Moss—the name beside the large house to the north. Henry had seen it in the distance, but had never approached.

"You're the one who left us the envelope in New York?"

Silvia gave a shy nod.

"If you wanted our help," Henry said, "why didn't you just talk to us? Why keep running away?"

Silvia shook her head. She pressed her hands together. "Please forgive me, Henry. I'm ashamed of it. I was afraid. Edward, he was a good friend of mine. Maybe my best friend. I was devastated when he died, but that hailstone story never sounded right to me. I wanted someone to look into it. I had never heard of a weather detective before—I didn't even know what one did—but it sounded like you and your uncle could help."

"Why didn't you just tell us?"

Silvia had a scared, regretful look in her eyes.

"I would have. I mean, I planned to. But I worry so much. I said to myself, 'If there really is a murderer, Silvia, he may live nearby. And if he finds out you hired a detective, he might come after you.' I don't expect you to understand, but I couldn't face that possibility. When I saw you and your uncle at Edward's place this morning, I followed you here."

As he listened, Henry found that he couldn't really hold Silvia's actions against her. After all, she was right. Whether Eugene Cook meant to commit murder or not, he had turned out to be pretty dangerous anyway. If Eugene had learned Silvia hired a detective, she might not have been safe.

Henry shrugged. "It's all right."

Silvia nodded graciously. Then, to Henry's surprise, she stepped forward, holding out her hand. "Before you go, I wanted to thank you. I'll be able to sleep better knowing that Edward's murderer has been caught."

After a short hesitation, Henry gripped the hand and shook it.

It felt nice. He might not have found his parents, but maybe he had done something good after all.

"You'll have to thank your uncle for me," Silvia said, readjusting herself. "Eugene will be in jail for a long time, I'm certain, but I still don't want him to see me here. He had quite the temper sometimes."

"Sure, I'll tell him."

Then, with nothing more to add, they both said goodbye. Henry watched Silvia—the woman who wasn't his mother after all—quietly disappear down the stairwell.

Turning, he found Rachel standing at the corner of the hallway.

"So that was the woman, huh?"

Henry sunk his hands into his pockets, walking toward Rachel. "Yeah. Not quite who I hoped for."

"I know. It'll be all right. Wherever your parents are, they still love you."

Rachel put her arm over Henry's shoulder and together they walked back into the crowded hallway. A handful of police led Eugene Cook away in handcuffs. He didn't look up as he lumbered past, but just stared down at the carpet, his nostrils plugged with cotton wool.

Farther down the hallway stood Kelvin. "Henry," Kelvin called out, running up to them. He looked flushed. "There you are."

"What is it?"

Kelvin's sharp gray eyes shimmered. "I wanted to apologize to you. I put you in a lot of danger on this trip, and I never meant to."

Vanessa and Clarence Willowby walked up to them as well. Henry shrugged his uncle's comment away. "It's okay. I know you didn't mean to."

But Kelvin didn't let the point drop. He knelt down, looking up to meet Henry's eyes. "No, it's not okay. I know things have been a little rough for us recently, but I'm your guardian, Henry. I may not be your father, but I'm supposed to protect you and do my best for you anyway. That's what guardian means: protector. I got angry when you went into Mr. Wrightly's house because I felt that I failed to keep you safe, and I failed again today. I got so caught up in solving this case that I put you in danger, so now it's my turn to apologize. Can you forgive me?"

Henry looked down at his uncle for several long seconds, kneeling there in his familiar paint-splattered overcoat. But in the end Henry couldn't help smiling. Even if his parents weren't around anymore, Kelvin was the best sort of family he could have hoped for.

"I forgive you. Most of it was my fault anyway." He got his uncle to his feet. "Besides, I think you're a great guardian."

Chapter Twenty-Three

Not an End, but a Beginning

With their paperwork done and witness statements taken, the last of the police soon packed up their things and left.

"We'll contact you, Mr. McCloud," they said, "if we need anything else."

It was then just past ten in the morning. Henry and Rachel went into her hotel room and sat on the bed together, and Kelvin had some private words with Vanessa and Clarence in the hall.

"Sorry about jumping into you again," Henry said. "You know, after Eugene grabbed me."

Rachel laughed. "I think I'll allow it, this time."

Kelvin, Vanessa, and Clarence soon appeared. Kelvin gave Clarence a nudge, and Clarence sat down heavily on the bed beside Rachel. He put a hand on her shoulder.

"I know this hasn't been much of a vacation, Rachel," he said. "Sorry we've been so busy."

Rachel shrugged. "It's all right, Dad. Gotta pay the bills, right?"

Vanessa smiled, getting them all to their feet. "How about, for the rest of the day, we all go to the beach?"

So, for the first time since she and her parents had arrived in Sandy Run, Rachel got to spend a day at the beach.

Rachel and Henry swam out into the water, bobbed up and down on the waves, fled from jellyfish, and looked for shells. The adults, after a timid jaunt into the cool shallows, relaxed in chairs on the sunbaked sand. Kelvin and Henry had checked out of the hotel earlier, but Kelvin decided they could stay in Sandy Run until after dinner. Rachel and her parents would be heading home the following morning, making the long drive back to Ohio.

But at last! No more arson and theft and murder! Henry liked a bit of intrigue, sure, but he'd had enough to last him a long time. As he looked at Rachel, treading water beside him, he only wished they didn't have to leave so soon.

Thankfully, summer days are long. And with the gradual, meandering patience of summer, the daylight lingered on.

Henry found himself sitting on the sand with Rachel late that afternoon, looking out over the rough surf and waves of the ocean. The sun hung lower now, but still brought warmth. In front of Henry and Rachel stood a mighty sand fortress they had built. Rachel dug the water-filled moats and Henry furnished it with seaweed.

Rachel leaned back on her hands, wiggling her fingers deep in the sand. She looked at the three adults a small distance away. "Don't think I'm being nosy, Henry, but there's something I wanted to ask about your uncle."

"Yeah? What is it?"

Rachel pressed her lips together. "Does he always talk about science so much? I mean, it's cool, but kind of strange."

Henry laughed. He looked at Kelvin, who lounged out of earshot in a beach chair, talking with Vanessa and Clarence with a book on his knee.

"Yeah, he's always like that," Henry said with a shrug. "He loves that sort of stuff. Used to be a professor. After a while, you start to appreciate it."

Henry intended to leave it at that, but he remembered something else. His uncle had once answered this very question for him.

"Actually, he told me one time," he said. Rachel leaned over, listening closely. "According to him, doing science is a lot like solving a mystery. It can be tricky at first, and you have to do a lot of investigating and sleuthing around, trying to see how everything fits together, but in the end it's satisfying to figure things out."

Rachel nodded, and Henry went on.

"Kelvin says the scientific method—you know, coming up with a hypothesis, then making tests to see if it's right or not—is pretty much just detective work. In both cases, you're looking for the truth."

Rachel turned her eyes to the sky. "So that's the reason. Doing science is another way of being a detective. I thought he was just being weird."

Henry laughed. "Well, he is weird. But he likes to tell me that, with science, the whole world is a mystery."

Henry stared out at the ocean as he said this. It stretched out before him, vast and strange. What else was out there? He imagined himself sailing out over that dark abyss, looking for answers like an explorer searching for new lands.

"A scientist is a detective and an adventurer," Kelvin had told him, "and the whole world is a mystery, just waiting to be explored."

Henry felt a warm hand on his own and suddenly returned to the beach. He looked over. Rachel's hand rested on top of his. His cheeks tingled hotly.

"Well, here's another mystery for you."

Saying this, she leaned over and kissed him square on the cheek. A warm, pleasant flash ran through Henry's whole body, starting at that spot and running like electricity all the way to his toes.

He couldn't help grinning like an idiot.

Leaning over, he kissed her back.

That evening, Henry felt thoroughly content even as he and Kelvin drove away from Sandy Run. Honestly, he couldn't help it. His cheek still tingled with that kiss.

Over dinner, he and Rachel had exchanged email addresses and promised to keep in touch.

"Rachel might even be able to visit New York sometime soon," Vanessa told Henry. "You could show her around the city."

Henry nodded, and soon came time to say goodbye. The sky hung darkly overhead. Kelvin gave Vanessa and Clarence a firm shake of the hand, and Rachel squeezed Henry in a tight hug.

"Take care, Henry," she told him.

"You too."

As they drove away, Henry waved at her through the window. Then, as the road stretched away from the town, he watched as all the lights of Sandy Run, and all of the mysteries still there, faded into the distance behind. He turned forward. Rachel's visit couldn't come soon enough.

Through the window, the stars began to come out, shining above the dark land rolling by. Kelvin's car bumped and gurgled beneath the inky expanse.

"By the way," Henry said to his uncle, "our client, Silvia Moss, says thanks."

A thin smile creased Kelvin's lips. "We should be thanking her. She's given our weather detective business a real start."

Henry nodded, happy to agree. This was a start. Gazing out the window, he couldn't even imagine what might come next.

Acknowledgements

It takes a village to write a book. The author would like to thank his family and friends for their help and support, Tony Broccoli and Dave Robinson for their scientific expertise, and Penny Noyce, Carrie Rogers, and Ian Graham Leask for their invaluable comments and criticisms during the revision process. Without these people, this book would not have been possible.

About the Author

Michael Erb fell in love with the weather while staring at the sky from his childhood home in North Carolina. He currently spends his time exploring past climates, thinking about the future, and collaborating with great scientists as he works toward his Ph.D. at Rutgers University. This is his first book, but Henry, Rachel, and Kelvin have many more adventures in store.

Now Available!

THE DESPERATE CASE OF THE
DIAMOND CHIP

By Pendred Noyce

When the Russian scientist Professor Gufov accuses Clinton of stealing his invention, all Mae and Clinton want to do is get away and work on their science project. But that's before a Dudette from the future tells them about the Galactic Academy of Science and sends them on a mission back in time. They break up a séance, escape from the Gestapo, jump from a plane, and learn how electronics work so they can tackle the mystery of the Russian scientist and recover the missing diamond chip.

Meet new scientists throughout history in

The Galactic Academy of Science.

Coming Soon!

THE FURIOUS CASE OF THE
FRAUDULENT FOSSIL

By Barnas Monteith

Benson and Anita meet a paleontologist at their local natural history museum. He tells them about his new find: a missing link between dinosaurs and birds. The students don't trust his findings, but they don't know how to prove he's up to no good. Then a Dude from the future sends them back in time to visit an ancient Chinese scientist, dig a sea monster out of a cliff, and outwit a fossil thief. Their new knowledge of paleontology will help them uncover the fraudulent fossil.

Meet new scientists throughout history in

The Galactic Academy of Science.

More science fun is on the horizon with

Tumblehome Learning

Whether you are interested in engineering, dinosaurs, space, biology, or other wonders of the universe, we have something for you. Check out our website for other books and experiments.

www.tumblehomelearning.com